ONE MORE GIFT

HOLLY JUNE SMITH

Contents

For anyone who puts *'pleasure'* at the top of their Christmas wishlist. Here's a double helping.

A Note From Holly

THANK YOU FOR READING *One More Gift*. I hope you enjoy it as much as I enjoyed writing it.

This is a fun MMF snowed-in holiday novella with low angst and high heat. However, there are mentions of divorce (amicable), and very brief discussions on whether or not to have children. If these are challenging for you, please take care.

It also contains:

- Toy play

- Restraint (to a chair, and to a table)

- Blindfolds

- Gags

- Light degradation

- Dominance/submission

- Bi awakening and discussions of sexuality

Happy holidays!

About the Author

Holly June Smith is a writer and romance addict who is constantly falling in love with fictional heroes and dreaming up new ones.

Holly is also a wedding celebrant who helps couples celebrate their beautiful real-life love stories.

Originally from the North East of Scotland, she now lives in Hertfordshire, England, with her partner, their two children, and a TBR that threatens to crush her in her sleep.

You can find her online @hollyjunesmith or join the Holly June Smith Reader Group on Facebook.

Chapter 1

Saskia

IT'S BEEN MONTHS SINCE I felt the exquisite stretch of a cock inside me.

A few hours more shouldn't matter, but suddenly I can't bear them.

"Are you sure you don't want me to pick you up from the airport?" I ask, balancing my phone between my ear and my shoulder as I slip a second bottle of Chablis into the fridge. "I don't mind."

"Absolutely sure," Henry says. "You stay nice and warm. Just make sure the fire is lit, and the wine is chilling."

I smile and press my lips together, leaning back to glance through the kitchen door to where the wood burner is roaring away in the living room. We've always been like this. In sync, on the same wavelength, even from the first day we met back at university.

"I'm one step ahead of you on both counts."

"Of course you are," he says warmly. "And can you maybe rustle something up so I can eat when I get there?"

My head snaps back. "Did you just *husband* me?"

"I beg your pardon?"

"That comment has extreme *get back in the kitchen, wench* vibes."

He bursts out laughing on the other end of the line. "You know I don't mean it like that, but I don't want to waste any time finding food in an airport when I land. I want to be there now."

My cheeks flush at his words. I want him here, too. We've been waiting far too long to be reunited. "Well, in that case, I'm sure I can rustle something up to keep you satisfied."

I can't be certain, but I'm sure I hear him growl. I bite the tip of my thumbnail between my teeth and my thighs squeeze together all on their own.

"My flight is boarding," he says, coughing to clear his throat. "I'll see you soon, darling."

Darling.

The word my ears most long to hear.

I already have Henry's favourite meal waiting to go in the oven, of course. A Shepherd's pie I prepared myself with local lamb and rosemary potatoes. He occasionally mentions how much he misses it, and that he's never found an acceptable substitute in New York City. Sometimes I taunt him with a photo of me cooking, and a tongue in cheek *'if you want it you'll have to come get it'* that we both know isn't about the food.

We'll be eating dinner a little later than usual, but I don't mind when it means he'll be here in the same room as me. I'll just need to keep my hands to myself while he eats and settles in. He'll be exhausted after such a long day of travelling, I'm sure, though he only has himself to blame for that.

He only decided to come back two days ago, amidst several confessions of longing, meaning the only flights left to London connected via Europe. Thankfully, things have gone smoothly in Amsterdam and my heart can relax a little further knowing he's one journey closer.

The last of the December sun is creeping low on the horizon, painting the living room in a golden haze. I set about transforming the place for the evening, flicking on lamps and lighting the scented candles on the coffee table.

Even though we're only staying for a short time, I wanted to make an effort for Henry. To give him a proper Christmas rather than one alone in his high-rise Manhattan apartment with takeout for dinner and the TV for company like last year.

I always go over the top with decorations here at the cottage. A forest of bottle-brush Christmas trees sit in a row on the mantlepiece, above knitted stockings adorned with our initials. There's a wreath on the door, and paper-chains hung from the ceiling, with plenty more to make.

Lights twinkle on the spruce I picked up from a nearby Christmas tree farm yesterday. While watching a film, I draped it with baubles and fairy lights; the tempo set to alternating twinkles. Simple and elegant, just how I like it.

This year has been anything but simple. We've spent it apart, with me living and working in London and him in New York. Even though he's always been just a phone call away, day or night, that doesn't mean we haven't been dealing with enormous change. We desperately need this precious time to reconnect, just the two of us, without outside influences demanding our time and energy.

I'm more nervous than I've let on, and much too fidgety to concentrate. I try to get comfortable in the armchair and read a book, but the words blur on the page. I consider a movie, but there's a strong chance I'll fall asleep, and I'd hate to look like a mess when he arrives. My phone buzzes on the dining table and I rush to grab it.

Henry: Just collected car. See you soon.

It's a thirty-minute drive without traffic, and there shouldn't be any at this hour. I do a sweep of the house to make sure everything is in order, even though I know it is. It's been a couple of months since anyone has stayed here, so I spent the day cleaning and freshening things up.

There are crisp, clean linens on the beds, the log basket by the fireplace is full, and the fridge brimming with ingredients for a Christmas feast. The wine rack is well stocked and, with the weather forecast predicting the first white Christmas in years, there's nothing left to do but hunker down and get reacquainted.

Chapter 2

Saskia

UPSTAIRS, I CHANGE OUT of my comfy clothes and into the outfit I've had planned for his arrival. Brand new lingerie underneath a black leather skirt, and a grey cashmere wrap top that makes my boobs the highlight of the outfit.

I'm a very tactile person. My favourite clothes, much like my favourite artworks, have texture and contrast. The juxtaposition of smooth leather and soft cashmere has me wanting to rub my hands all over myself.

Hopefully that means Henry won't be able to keep his hands to himself either. I want him to want me so much he can't bear it.

Shoes are forbidden in the cottage since I had the carpets replaced, so I wear fluffy pink slippers instead. The ensemble has a unique vibe, but with any luck, I won't be wearing any of it for long.

In the bathroom I reapply my lipstick, blot it with a tissue, and finish off the look with a spritz of Tom Ford perfume. The name, *Lost Cherry*, makes me blush. What a fitting scent for us two.

Finally, while pacing between the kitchen and living room, I see headlights on the approach. The only other vehicles that come along this road are farm traffic and they're done for the day, so I know it must be him. I check my hair in the mirror by the door, take a deep breath and adjust my top, positioning it delicately on my shoulders so it looks like it could slip down at any second. I give the girls one last nudge together in my bra, and I'm ready for my man.

My heart rate ratchets up as I contemplate how soon is too soon to open the door. I don't want to seem desperate even though every fibre of my body is thrumming with need.

I open just in time to see him parking on the driveway area at the end of the small front garden, and he hops out, his smile clear even in the darkness.

"Good evening, Mr Stone," I call out.

"Miss Hatton," he says with a smile, slamming the car door and rushing up the path to the house. I haven't been Miss Hatton for a long time, but that's what he used to call me back when we first met.

I welcome him with open arms, and his wrap tight around me, crushing me against his chest. I feel the warmth of him against my cheek, breathe in the scent of his cologne, and everything softens when he sighs into my hair, lifting me onto my tiptoes.

"There's my girl."

I'm so happy I could cry.

He sets me back down and pulls away to get a proper look at my face. His kiss lands on the corner of my mouth where my smile is wide. It's too close to be a mistake. It's a promise of what's coming.

"Fuck, I've missed you," he says, his gorgeous green eyes flitting back and forth between mine. It's as if he's staring into my soul, sweeping away my worries and replacing them with reassuring thoughts.

We'll be OK. We'll finally be OK.

I believe him. His expression is beautiful, the porch light illuminating both him and the soft flakes that drift in from the dark December sky.

"I've missed you too. Come in before you get cold."

"It smells incredible in here," he says, stepping further into the warmth. "The food, and you."

This is what I've been longing for. Him. His words. The intimate familiarity we've lost in our time apart.

"The place looks great," he says, looping one arm around my shoulder as he looks around the living room. It doesn't take long since the front door opens straight into this room, as is common in these old cottages.

An original fireplace lines one wall, with comfy sofas positioned around it in an L-shape. Stacks of firewood are piled neatly in one alcove, and the other contains the television, completely out of proportion for such a small space, but perfect for snuggly movie marathons.

Behind the longest sofa is a dining area with a table and chairs, and past that is the door to the small kitchen that has everything I need to cook the kind of hearty, nourishing meals one craves in the middle of the countryside.

"You got a tree?"

"I did." I smile against his side. He's finally here. "Are you ready to eat?"

"Would you mind terribly if I took a quick shower?"

"Of course not. Everything's ready. I just need to steam the greens."

"Let me grab my bag from the car and I'll be as fast as I can." He opens the door to leave, then darts back towards me, taking my face in his big hands and dropping a kiss to my forehead. My cheeks mourn the loss of his warmth.

He comes back a few seconds later, locking the door behind him. He bypasses the living room to take the stairs to the upper level, grinning the whole time. In the kitchen, I turn on the hob and hover, enjoying the sounds of the house with two people in it.

Upstairs, two double bedrooms share a bathroom, and I can hear him singing to himself as he turns on the water. The cottage is small, but the perfect size for when I need to escape the craziness of life in London.

I bought it after I made my first million pound commission, a huge milestone for any art dealer. It captured my heart the moment I saw the exterior and immediately reminded me of the cottage where Cameron Diaz falls in love with Jude Law in *The Holiday*.

The interior left a lot to be desired, but after negotiating a decent-price for a cash purchase, I had plenty of money left to bring it up to my standards.

I've left the original wooden beams and window frames untouched, but painted the place off-white throughout, with cream carpets and soft furnishings. It's completely different to our flat in London, where the theme is much more reflective of my taste in art, but that's always been the point. The cottage is art itself. A place for peace and relaxation.

And fucking each other's brains out without any neighbours to hear you scream.

Henry reappears wearing faded black jeans, slung low on his hips, and a tight ribbed top, with the sleeves pushed up his forearms.

"Better?"

"Reborn," he says, shaking his damp, dark hair like a Labrador, then raking his fingers through it and pushing it back. The man has always been handsome, and he's only getting better with age. My lips curl into a smile as I pour him a glass of wine, sliding it across the counter. His hand catches my wrist, and tugs me towards him until I land against his chest with a soft thud. "You look so good."

He holds me close, one palm stroking up and down my back, the other tangling in my hair. I feel his touch everywhere, dancing through my nerves, lighting a fire inside me.

I've needed this so much. Needed *him*. Wanted him. Yearned for so long, and now finally he's here, and all my Christmas wishes are about to come true.

Chapter 3

Henry

MY RESTRAINT IS HANGING on by a thread. Kissing her is all I've been craving for weeks, all I've thought about on both flights it took me to get here. When I cup her chin and tilt her head to look up at me, the pull to press my lips to hers is magnetic.

If I had my way, Saskia would be naked and on her third orgasm by now, but the whole point of this trip is to take our time to reconnect, to figure things out, to settle into each other's company after so long apart.

The fear that I'll scare her off is real, and I can hold back a little longer. There's all the time in the world now, for me to take her in, gaze into her eyes, free to look without shame or guilt. My thumb caresses her cheek, while the other strokes her back, my hand working over her body instinctively.

I'm in no rush, and I know for certain she'll be very worth the wait.

Saskia has always been stunning. Long limbs, toned from years of getting up at the crack of dawn to lace up her trainers and pound the London pavements. At first glance, you might mistake her elegance for the fragility of a delicate woman, but those who know her best know how strong she is, both physically and mentally.

Her facial features are perfectly symmetrical, framed by the long strands that have fallen loose from the ponytail I'm now wrapping around my fist. Her eyes stay locked with mine, shimmering, waiting.

I've always loved those bright blue eyes, that cute button nose, and the way her cheeks flush when she's flirting. Just as they are now.

In the summer she tans easily, her skin turning a golden brown that I've always wanted to sink my teeth into. In the winter months, she's a different story, the quintessential English rose. The layers of her top have me feeling like Saskia is a gift waiting to be unwrapped.

My hands graze over the tight leather skirt that hugs her peachy backside, leaving little to the imagination. I want to sink my teeth into that, too, but my fingers will suffice for now. I grip both cheeks with a firm squeeze, making her yelp and press her tits, firm and high, harder against my chest.

Oh yes, she's a fucking dream, and I'm the luckiest man on the planet to have her all to myself this week.

My mouth drops to the expanse of bare flesh at her shoulder and her slender fingers curl around the back of my neck. I'm confident we could have each other naked in under ten seconds.

"You're so beautiful, darling."

The words barely scratch the surface of things I want to say to her. And I will.

Soon.

The oven timer dings, and she releases me from her hug. "Take a seat at the table and I'll plate everything up."

For now, the least I can do is enjoy the delicious dinner she's cooked for us. Saskia's always been a brilliant cook. She arrived on her first day at university with a sharp set of knives and a head full of recipes, and I've been the grateful recipient of many of her meals ever since.

She's taught me a few things over the years, though my days in New York are so long and busy, I can't say I cook often. I hope to change that this weekend, and return the favour, looking after her the way she's always looked after me.

The table seats six, far too big for the small dining area in her little country cottage, but I know when she's out here, she likes to pass the time with a jigsaw puzzle. Something to keep her hands busy and away from her phone so she doesn't slip into the habit of working all hours of the day.

In New York, I go to basketball games to unwind, but each to their own. She won't need a puzzle this week, and she sure as hell won't be emailing anyone on my watch.

She takes the seat across from me, and I'm grateful for the chance to sit and look at her while we eat.

"Is this Shepherd's pie?" A ridiculous question when I know full well I'm staring at a plate of my favourite meal.

"Sure is," she says, biting into a piece of broccoli with a satisfied grin on her face.

"When I asked you to rustle something up, I meant like a sandwich."

She shrugs like this was nothing. "It was already in the oven."

That's Saskia for you. She has the purest heart of anyone I've ever met and if you're in her life, you know you're lucky to have her.

"You're too good to me, you know that, right?"

It should feel strange being here with her after so long apart, but it's anything but. My foot rubs against hers underneath the table, and unlike previous occasions, she doesn't pull away.

We lose ourselves in talk of art over dinner, giving updates on our clients' recent purchases, name-dropping in a competitive game of one-upmanship we've been playing ever since we took our first positions as art dealers. Who's buying art under a fake name, who's splurging on pieces for mistresses, who might be going bankrupt in the new year. Of course, confidentiality is key in our world, and we're often required to sign NDAs, but there's nobody I trust with my secrets more than Saskia.

When we finish, she carries our dishes through to the sink, but I follow behind her, wrapping my arms around her waist to pull her away.

"I'll wash up in the morning while you lie in," I murmur against her neck. From this angle, I have a perfect view right down the front of her sweater. Those perfect tits, full and pressed together in whatever bra she's chosen.

The ties of her top are looped around her waist and fastened in a neat bow at the back. I want to tug the ends free and watch the fabric fall from her skin, but that can wait.

She moans softly, tilting her head to give me more access to her smooth, delicate skin. The urge to lick her, suck my mark into her flesh, bite down just hard enough to make her whimper is all-consuming. For now, I settle for breathing, deep and slow, right above the surface of her skin.

Saskia has always loved the thrill of anticipation. You can see it in the way she works, the flush of colour in her cheeks right before she seals a deal. I've seen it many times over the years, though not nearly enough lately.

I wonder how high I can get her just from the anticipation of my touch. How squirmy and desperate she would get before she begged me for more.

Nuzzling my face against the side of her head, I inhale the clean scent of her shampoo. "Let's sit in the living room."

She practically whines, which only spurs me on to make her wait even longer.

While I top up our wine glasses, Saskia bends to add a couple more logs to the fire. I suck in air through my teeth. Her body looks like heaven, and this outfit is a real fucking test of my patience.

It's better suited to a day in the office than a relaxing weekend in a cosy remote cottage, but I know she's made an effort for me, even if she's trying to pass it off as casual. Mark my words, she'll be extremely comfortable soon, and hopefully won't be wearing much more than one of my t-shirts for the foreseeable future.

My cock twitches beneath my jeans. That's my core memory of her, the morning after we first slept together all those years ago. Her legs, unfathomably long, disappearing up underneath the t-shirt that skimmed the tops of her thighs as she climbed back into my lap. Not a scrap of clothing underneath.

Fuck.

I think about it a lot more than a decent man should.

I take a seat on the longer of the two sofas, the one that sits in the middle of the room, facing the fireplace. This is a room that she designed with love and attention, a perfect escape from busy city life.

Saskia hovers, fiddling with a decoration on the tree. She's understandably cautious now that I'm here. We've grown up, found our way in the real world. We have more to lose now.

She takes a seat at the other end of the sofa, kicking off her fluffy slippers, then tucking her legs up underneath her. I pat my thigh and she rolls her eyes, stretching her legs out until her feet are in my lap.

"That's better," I say, taking a sip of my wine and settling the glass down on the coffee table. I smooth my palm down from her shin to the top of her foot, wrapping my hand around it and pressing into the underside with the pad of my thumb.

Saskia groans lightly, sinking further down against the sofa cushions. I keep working my thumb along her arch, watching how the rest of her body responds.

"How was your flight?"

"I don't want to talk about my flight." I track my gaze from her foot all the way up her legs until I watch her throat bob.

"What do you want to talk about, then?"

Her question is barely a whisper, but in the quiet of the remote house, I hear her loud and clear.

"I don't want to talk at all, actually."

I don't want there to be any awkwardness between us, but with so much buildup, I'm talking *years* of tension, I think we have to push straight past it. I'm certain we both know what we want, even if we haven't been able to say it out loud for some time. We need to break down our walls so we can put ourselves back together again, anew. I can't dance around it anymore.

"Come here, sweetheart."

Sweetheart.

That's new, but it feels like butter in my mouth, and I love it.

She's smiling too much to move, hiding her mouth behind her thumb the way she does when she's nervous. She has nothing to be nervous about with me, so I cup one hand behind her knee and reach the other around her waist, lifting her into my lap with ease.

She lands with a moan, her skirt riding up her thighs as she sinks down into me. It's impossible to suppress a moan of my own when my hands find their home on top of her bare legs.

"Is this OK?"

"Very OK," she nods, resting her hands on my shoulders.

"Good."

My girl, at long last, is right where she belongs. I tip my head back against the sofa cushions so I can get a better look at her. Her eyes, full and bright even in the low light, that pouty bottom lip that drives me fucking nuts when she tugs it behind her teeth. I don't want to be the guy that just stares at her tits, but I know they're right fucking there and if I lower my gaze just a fraction, I'll never be able to look away.

Please.

I see it written in her eyes.

There's always been this thing between us, her reading my mind, answering without words, but some things need to be said out loud so there's no room for mistakes.

"I want you so fucking much, Sass." My thumbs stroke soft, lazy circles around the inside of her thighs. Her head slumps forward, and I feel the toned muscles twitching. Knowing the effect I'm having on her gets me even harder, and when she rocks her hips slightly, I wonder if she feels what she's doing to me.

"Me too."

"Let me hear you ask for what you want."

"I... I..." I pinch the inside of her thigh and she yelps. "I want you to kiss me."

It's the very least I can do. Sitting up straight, I boost her closer to me, one hand under her perfect ass, the other tipping her chin until her mouth is just millimetres away from mine. This pretty, fiery, passionate thing. It was the very first thing I loved about her as I followed the sound of her laugh across a crowded lecture hall.

She sinks even lower and her lips land on mine, electricity zipping between us until she opens for my tongue and—

Bright light beams through the window, dazzling us both. She pulls back, shielding her eyes from the onslaught.

"What on earth...?" she says, climbing off me, straightening her skirt from where it's ridden up high.

Saskia peels back the curtains, and the room darkens again as the driver kills the engine. I move to stand behind her, wondering who would be visiting at this hour, in the middle of nowhere.

A heavy sigh pours out of her when the car door opens and a shadowy figure steps out into fresh, crisp snowfall.

"Who is it?" I ask, and she tips her head back against my chest and groans.

"It's my husband."

Chapter 4

Saskia

IN THE DOORWAY WHERE he once carried me over the threshold, Casper slides one fingertip into the spot where my top crosses into a v-shape at my cleavage. He pulls it towards him and takes a brazen peek.

"Maroon," he says with a wicked smile. "That's fucking hot."

I yank his hand away and plaster my back to the wall. "It's new."

Henry hangs back on the other side of the living room, and for some reason, I really need him to know this. To know I made a special effort for him. I haven't thrown on old underwear someone else has already seen and enjoyed.

"So I see. I wouldn't forget your tits in a bra like that."

Casper laughs, and I bite back a smile. He has always been a relentless flirt. It's what drew me to him in the first place. It's impossible to pretend it doesn't affect me anymore, even though right now I want to scream at him for being the biggest cockblock on the planet. Turning up just as Henry and I were about to get, shall we say, reacquainted, was not part of my elaborately crafted plan for Christmas.

"What are you doing here?" I ask.

"I thought you would be in London for the holidays. It seems I was mistaken." He gestures out to the driveway where three cars are now lined up. "And it looks like you have company?"

"I'm sure I told you I'd be here, Casper. And Henry just arrived from New York," I say, thumbing over my shoulder. "We're staying here until the new year."

"Oh." His tone is curt, and I can't get a proper read on his reaction in the dim light of the doorway. "How festive."

He shrugs out of his coat, hanging it on top of mine like he owns the place, which I guess he technically does. Well, half owns.

With me.

His soon to be ex-wife.

"Henry, my buddy," he booms, stepping into the room.

"Shoes off the carpet," I yell, and he does his best impression of a naughty schoolboy, quickly tip-toeing back to slip out of his Italian leather brogues.

"Come here, big man, it's good to see you."

Casper and Henry do that weird bro-hug thing, where they each have one arm around the waist and the other above the shoulder. It always makes me think they're about to wrestle, which, given the circumstances of us all being in the same room again, is not outside the realm of possibility.

Casper is a stark contrast to Henry's casual vibe, but handsome as always, in his trademark black jeans and black t-shirt. He's definitely not dressed for winter in rural Hertfordshire, which is no surprise given I thought he was spending Christmas with his family.

"Good to see you too, Casper," Henry says. He steps back, hands plunging into his pockets as his eyes find mine across the room.

The timing could not be worse. My underwear is soaked from the anticipation of the man I've wanted for years, finally touching me again. Tonight was supposed to be the start of... well, I don't know what exactly, but a new beginning for the two of us.

Casper flops down in the middle of the sofa, leaning forward to pick up my glass of wine. He brings it to his nose and inhales deeply.

"This is French," he scoffs, setting it back down.

"Don't be such a snob," I say from where I'm still frozen to the spot by the doorway. "I thought you were in Italy?"

"I had a last-minute meeting with a buyer in Mayfair. He wants to commission six pieces for his new penthouse. I figured this place would be empty."

"You couldn't find a hotel?"

"Of course I could," he laughs, stretching his arms out across the back of the sofa cushions. "But this place has such happy memories for me. For us, my angel. I wanted to visit one last time."

He turns to look at Henry and even from where I stand behind him, I can tell he has a shit-eating grin plastered on his face. Henry looks as confused as I am, swaying slightly on the spot, unsure whether to sit, stand, or leave.

I really don't want him to leave, and I'm not about to let our precious time together be ruined by some pathetic pissing contest because my husband has a jealous streak.

Ex-husband!

"Well, where are you going to stay?" I ask, rounding the sofa with my hands on my hips. "There are only two bedrooms here."

Henry glances sideways. We hadn't spoken about it implicitly, but I think it's pretty obvious he was going to stay in my room. With me.

Despite that, I don't want the man I'm in the process of divorcing to know I've invited another man, my oldest friend no less, to share my bed.

It's ridiculous. We separated almost a year ago. I'm allowed to sleep with other people, as is he. I just didn't expect the first time I'd have sex with someone else in fifteen years to be while he was in the house with us.

"We shared a bed for years, angel. I'm sure we can manage one more night."

The three of us look back and forth at each other in a sort of stand-off until Casper breaks the silence with a laugh.

"I am teasing. I can sleep on the sofa. Henry, you'll have the guest bedroom and my wife can have our bedroom to herself."

"*My* bedroom," I correct him.

"If you say so. Is there anything to eat?" he says, smirking up at me. I could punch him in his beautiful mouth.

Our separation has been as civil as they come, and although we still speak regularly, it's been a few months since we've seen each other in person. I'm furious at him for turning up here looking so gorgeous.

One man aging like a fine wine is a treat, two is torture, and I don't know where to look.

There's no sane way through this situation except retreating to our separate corners of the cottage and surviving the night. It's late, and if we can just get through the next few hours, Casper will leave, and Henry and I can get back on track, just a little later than expected.

"You know where the kitchen is. I'm going to go to bed."

"Sleep well, my beautiful angel," Casper calls after me.

"You're leaving in the morning," I yell back down the stairs.

"As you wish." I hear him laughing, then making his way to the kitchen.

In my bedroom, I strop about my room as I change into snuggly a top and bottoms, the exact opposite of what I had planned to spend the evening in. I packed them to wear while curled up on the sofa, watching Christmas movies underneath a blanket.

Henry's suitcase is sitting at the foot of my bed, and the sight of it, closed and unpacked, makes me want to cry. He *was* going to stay in here. Obviously he was. We didn't even need to discuss it.

There's a soft knock at the door, which can only be Henry. Casper would never bother knocking.

"Come in."

"Hey, just came to grab my stuff and check on you." He closes the door quietly behind him. "Are you OK?"

"I'm fine," I say, losing my battle with hanging my skirt in the tiny wardrobe in the corner. "I'm just... I'm so sorry, Henry. I don't know what he's doing here and I'm pretty fucking angry about it, to be honest."

"Hey, it's OK. Don't worry about it."

"I'm not worried, I'm just frustrated. This was supposed to be... this is..." I wave my hands back and forth between us. I don't have the words for whatever this is yet. "I was really looking forward to spending time here, just the two of us."

Henry closes the space between us and pulls me into his arms, his chin resting on the top of my head. My arms loop around his strong back, and my body lights up being so close to him. I want this, this and more, all week long.

"We're good, Sass. You and me? We can handle setbacks," he whispers into my hair, and it's all the reassurance I need. "You should get some sleep. He'll be gone in the morning, and you and I can pick up where we left off. OK?"

I lift my chin to catch the look of promise in his eyes. Promise and hunger. His big hands stroke up and down my biceps and I never want him to stop touching me.

"OK. I'm so sorry. I had no idea he would be here, I promise. We're well and truly over, and he knows that. I don't know why he's saying *'my wife'* and all that shit."

"That's just the way he is, but honestly, I've waited a long fucking time for you. It's already late. I can wait a few more hours." He smiles down at me, gives my bum a hard squeeze, then raises his hands in mock apology. "Sorry, I really needed that. To tide me over."

I want to kiss him, but if I do, I don't think I'd be able to stop myself from touching him and taking things further. There are so many things I do with him. Tonight was supposed to end with me screaming his name. Let the man downstairs hear me for all I care.

Henry presses a kiss to my forehead and my heart aches to watch him leave.

"See you tomorrow," he says, one hand still on the doorknob.

"Tomorrow."

Chapter 5

Saskia

An hour later, I'm tossing and turning beneath layers of blankets, thinking of all the things I want to say to Henry, and all the things I want to scream at Casper.

My bedroom door creaks open, soft light spilling in from the hallway. I sit up, my eyes adjusting to the intrusion, but I don't need vision to identify the man sneaking into my bedroom in the middle of the night.

His large frame fills the room, his head almost skimming the low ceiling. I've lost count of the amount of times he's hit his head on something in this old house.

"What do you want, Casper?"

"I've come to make amends."

I pull my blankets up higher as he stalks towards me, taking a seat on the edge of the bed.

"You're not sleeping in here," I hiss, leaning to switch the bedside lamp on.

Alone in the dark with my ex-husband is a dangerous place to be. My body betrays my mind far too easily.

"I know that, but I can't sleep until I tell you I'm sorry. I swear, I didn't mean to intrude on your plans with your friend." He takes my hand in his palm, gently stroking the back of it.

He has always had beautiful hands, well-groomed, but calloused from hours spent holding a paintbrush. To witness him use them in his work has always been a joy, to watch them bring pleasure even more so. When I don't pull away, he turns my hand over and begins massaging my palm.

Some women like a long soak in the bath to unwind at the end of a long day, others prefer a foot rub. One of the best things about coming home to the London flat we shared was him pulling me into his lap on the sofa and soothing the tension out of my hands while we caught up about our days.

Eventually our hands would separate, the tips of mine tracing long, slow lines up and down the veins in his forearms. Sometimes his would slip beneath my waistband and tease me through my underwear. Other times, he'd flip me over and spread me across his lap, tug my skirt up and—

"Henry is here," he sighs, snapping me out of my hazy trip down memory lane. My eyes flick up to his.

"Yes. He is."

"So it's time?"

How can I explain why Henry is here when we haven't even had the chance to talk amongst ourselves yet?

"Angel, I am not a stupid man. Yes, I am often blinded by your beauty..." he tucks a piece of hair behind my ear and leans in close. "But I see everything that goes on in your mind."

It's true, nobody knows me better than Casper. He has been with me for so many years. For all the successes and failures, the dreams and desires. He's seen me at my best and worst, in sickness and in health, in all those things we vowed we'd mean forever.

"He has always had a special place in your heart. I knew this would happen one day."

His eyes lock with mine and I feel stripped bare.

If Casper De Luca knows me well, so does Henry Stone. He's been my best friend for years, always by my proverbial side, even when we've been living on opposite sides of the Atlantic.

"Truly, I didn't mean to interrupt your reunion."

"It's fine," I relent. "I thought I'd told you we would be here."

"So you forgive me?" he says, batting his eyelashes.

"Yes, I forgive you, as long as you promise to leave in the morning."

"After breakfast?" he says, patting my leg through the blankets. "You'll make me pancakes, I think."

"Fine, after pancakes."

"Seeing as I am here. Shall we have one last fuck?" he says with a wink, hopping up to straddle me on top of the covers.

"You are unbelievable," I laugh, shoving him away. "You've had about twelve one last fucks. We agreed to stop doing that."

My pussy betrays me though, muscle memory kicking in, and I clench around nothing, throbbing at the thought of having him inside me again.

Sex with Casper was always incredible, even after fifteen years together. Unlike many couples, that's not the reason we broke up. If anything, it's the reason we stayed together far longer than we should have.

The night we met, at a gallery opening in Chelsea, he brought me to orgasm in a taxi on the way home, and then fucked me on the hallway floor of his apartment. I'd had good sex before, but Casper operated on a different level. Nobody had ever touched me that way, ever anticipated my needs or emptied my brain like he did. He made me feel alive.

We were two hot young things with the sort of sexual chemistry people write books about. We pushed each other's limits and rarely made it as far as the bed in those early days.

Everyone assumed we'd burn out as fast as we'd begun, but there was a ring on my finger within six months, and after a June wedding at his grandmother's villa in Italy, we spent the entirety of our honeymoon naked.

No, unfortunately, our downfall was not in the bedroom, but in our values and dreams, something we'd failed to learn about each other when we'd been too preoccupied with making each other come.

I turned thirty, and the questioning began. When would we start a family? When would I give up work? When would we move to Italy? When, when, when.

His personality shift horrified me. My work was my life, and still is. My husband was an astonishing, boundary-breaking artist. Who had replaced him with this traditional family man?

Soon it became clear we had very different expectations of what our future together looked like. I don't dislike children, but I've never felt drawn to having my own. I like my life, and my work, and my freedom far too much. I don't care if that's selfish.

Three years later, it was all we talked about. Except it was more arguing than talking. Casper approached it with the same fiery passion he approached everything in life, bombarding me with reasons we'd be happier in Italy, telling me how beautiful I'd be with his baby in my belly.

His reasons were good for him, but the harder he pushed, the less I wanted it. We started avoiding each other. I'd stay late at work, or he'd fly to Europe for weeks at a time, seeking inspiration for his next piece of art. Once upon a time, I'd been all the inspiration he needed.

When he came home, we'd take our frustrations out on each other in the bedroom. Passionate, aggressive sex that left us in a scramble of bedsheets with marks on our skin. I'd be lying if I said I didn't like it, but then he's always brought a touch of deviance out in me.

"You know it would be a good time." He pitches his voice lower. The bastard. He knows what that voice does to me. "I know we cannot give each other everything we want, but I want to give you everything I can. Fulfil all those last fantasies."

"We've had fifteen years of fulfilling fantasies," I tell him. "I think that's plenty."

"Not all of them, though."

His fingers and thumb stroke down my cheeks to cup my chin. His eyes are dark with desire, and I know he's thinking about one in particular, a deeply held desire he's never been able to satisfy alone.

Heat pools deep in my core at the thought of it. Of hands, of mouths, of moans upon moans. The hedonistic allure of being worshipped and used, filled and fulfilled, over and over and—

"You need to leave."

I swallow hard and push one hand against his chest. He wraps his fingers around my wrist, tugging me up against him.

Over his shoulder, I see the door creak open again, and I scramble out of his arms.

Oh, shit.

"Saskia, is everything alright?" Henry asks.

"Of course. She is fine," Casper says, but everything is not alright. I know how this looks. "Come in, my friend."

Henry lurks in the doorway, and I shrug, the only way I can think to reassure the love of my life when he's just caught my ex-husband on top of me in bed.

"I was just leaving." Casper climbs off me, then bends to press a kiss to my forehead. It's sweet and tender, and not like him at all. "She's all yours."

"*What the fuck?*" Henry mouths at me as Casper passes him.

"Actually," Casper pauses, dropping his hand on Henry's shoulder. "On second thoughts…"

He makes his way over to the chair by my dressing table. Pulling it out, he twists it to face the bed and sits. Crossing one ankle over his knee, he leans back and stares up at Henry.

"Perhaps I should stay."

Chapter 6

Casper

I HAVE DONE SOME pretty depraved things to my wife in our time together, and she to me, but my biggest regret, sexually speaking, is that I've never seen her with another man.

If this is to be the last time she and I will sleep under the same roof, I don't see why we can't give each other one more gift. An epic send off, before we go our separate ways.

Henry looks confused—am I coming or going—but I think he'll get the hint soon enough. One beautiful woman, two virile men, a bed big enough for three in a remote cottage with no neighbours. What are we supposed to do, play Monopoly?

"I'll give you two some space," Henry says, but I grab his wrist so he can't make it past the door. He looks down at where I grip him, his jaw ticking.

"Don't leave."

"What are you doing?" Saskia asks, sitting up taller. Her long blonde hair falls in loose waves over her shoulders, and even without make-up, she's a natural beauty.

Heat from the fire downstairs has warmed the room, but the temperature often dips overnight. Without me here to keep her warm, she's dressed in a plain black, long-sleeved top. I can just make out the curve of her breasts as my eyes trace up to her delicate collarbone and the face that's glaring right at me.

I ignore her and gesture at the bed. "Take a seat, Henry."

"I, er..." Henry fumbles. I've never known him to be a weak man, but I think we're about to find out what he's really made of.

"Casper," Saskia pleads.

"I said sit down," I bark, and Henry's head snaps back. His eyes burn into mine, but when I release his arm, he does as he's told, moving to perch by her side. Saskia pulls her knees up to her chest underneath the blankets.

They look good together, I can't lie. He's about the same height as me, but not as broad, with a thick head of brown hair and kind eyes. He's got that classic British charm that's served him well in New York, though he hasn't picked up an accent in all his time living there.

He has a quiet confidence, but right now he looks nervous as hell. I watch his chest rise and fall, his thick fingers spread out on his thighs as he no doubt wonders what to do with his hands.

"What's going on here?" Henry asks, and I cock my head to one side and stare him down.

"If you want to take my wife from me, I need to know she'll be satisfied."

"Hey now," he snaps, standing up and looking back and forth between us. "This is not what that is. Nobody is taking anyone from anyone. She's free to make her own decisions. Right?"

She looks up at him with adoration in her eyes, the way she used to look at me.

"Right," she says.

"You might think she's free to make her own decisions, but we made vows. Her pussy belongs to me."

"What the fuck, Casper?" Saskia yells. I burst out laughing and slap my thigh.

"I am just kidding," I tell him. "But I know every inch of her body, every fantasy in that brilliant brain."

Saskia is livid, exactly the reaction I want from her. We may have mutually decided to end our marriage, but nobody could say it wasn't fucking fun turning our blazing arguments into furious sex. She's wild when she's angry, and sex is her preferred way of letting her feelings out. Anger at me, at her clients, at the world.

She never had an angry word to say about him, though. He's her port in a storm.

I pull my chair closer to the end of the bed. "My wife is a very sexual person, Henry. Did you know this about your friend? She's a busy lady, stressful job, pain in the ass husband who's constantly pissing her off."

Saskia bites back her smile, but I can tell she wants to laugh. Can tell she's already caught up with where I intend for this to lead, too. Unlike Henry, whose neck is throbbing, hands curled into tight fists by his sides. If I didn't know better, I'd think I was about to get knocked out.

"She needs someone who can take care of her at the end of a long day. Someone who can help her relax, worship and manipulate her body until her head is empty. Are you sure you're the man for the job?"

Henry stands with his hands on his hips, the outline of his erection clearly visible through his pyjama pants. "Yes, I am."

"Go on then. Take care of her."

"Excuse me?"

I sit up taller, linking my fingers, then dropping my elbows to my knees. "Get on the bed and take care of my wife the way she needs to be taken care of."

Saskia shifts into the centre of the mattress, the subtle permission he needs. Henry sits beside her, reaching for her hand. "Are you OK with this?"

"I am if you are," she whispers. She squeezes his hand reassuringly, and my erection throbs against my zipper. I knew she'd be game.

They gaze into each other's eyes, and I don't know how he's held himself back this long. If I had her permission to touch her, I wouldn't need any further encouragement. My cock would be buried in one of her perfect holes by now.

What Henry gets up to in New York is none of my business, but while this is new for me and my wife, I suspect it is for him, too. Maybe direction is what Henry needs.

"Show me how you kiss her."

"I... what?" Henry falters, and I wonder if maybe he's not up for this after all.

"What's the matter? Don't you want to kiss her?"

"I do," he says, shifting closer when she angles her body towards him. He cups her face in his hands, eyes never leaving hers while he answers me. "Desperately. I just didn't think you'd be here when I did it for the first time."

"What's the problem? You've kissed her before."

His head spins towards me. "You know about that?"

Chapter 7

Casper

HENRY HAS DONE A good job of maintaining his position as her best friend all these years, never overstepping boundaries or blurring lines. My wife never looked at another man in all the years we were together. She was mine until she wasn't, but I have always known there was unfinished business between them.

"I know everything there is to know about this woman, Henry."

He looks back at Saskia, and even in the dim light, I see her eyes sparkling. His palm settles on her cheek and she nuzzles into his touch, cupping his hand with her own.

"We shared our pasts, but he knows we're just friends," she says. Henry's throat rumbles at her poor choice of words and she grabs his arm with both hands. "*Were* just friends. Not now. He knows this is… we are…"

I roll my eyes as she stumbles over her words. I'm not here to witness their declarations of love, though I expect I interrupted them before they had the chance to really get into it.

"She loved it, you know? The way you fucked her. *'Tender and special'*, she called it."

I remember the night we spent together in our old apartment, bonding over whisky and our sexual experiences. She had an innocence back then, one I quickly stripped away.

"I got hard just from the way she described it, you know? Thinking about her straddling you in your dorm room. Thinking about you stretching her open for the first time. You were a lucky man to be her chosen one."

She tips her face up towards him, and I can practically feel how much she aches for him from the other side of the room. Henry regards her with a reverence that truly is beautiful to witness. She is angelic, gripping his shoulders while her body sways towards him.

"I was lucky," he breathes. "I *am* lucky."

Needing no further encouragement, Saskia inches forward, eyes squeezing shut when their lips press together.

They hold each other like that for a few seconds, then Henry pulls back, tucks her hair behind her ear, and searches her expression for approval. I appreciate the show of respect, but he already has her permission. Little is off limits with Saskia. I know she'd let him take anything he wanted from her right now.

She moans, sinking further into his hold when his tongue strokes into her mouth. They kiss with a hunger that has my cock swelling, even more when his hands land on her waist and slide up underneath her top.

"Doesn't she feel incredible?"

"She does," he says softly, angling his face to suck her lip between his teeth.

"What a shame you didn't get to see the lingerie she chose for you. It was very pretty."

My wife's hands stroke up and down his arms. It's exciting to see her in this state of need from a different perspective, with a different man.

My pleasure has always been heightened by witnessing hers. I've lost count of the number of times I've walked into a room, clocked the desire written all over her face, and gotten instantly hard. Nothing pushes me over the edge like that moment where her mouth falls open on a silent scream, and her body tightens and trembles beneath me.

For a long time, I believed I should be the only one to make her feel that way, but my fantasies have often turned to the vision I see before me now. Her lost in pleasure derived from elsewhere.

Saskia has always loved to play games, and has quite the exhibitionist kink.

My cock throbs at the memory of nights in our London apartment. The many occasions when I returned from my studio to find her laid out on our marital bed in nothing but lingerie and a blindfold. Even without words, her message was clear.

'Watch me.'

In silence, I'd take a front-row seat for the most spectacular show on earth, and hold back while she stroked and teased herself. Sometimes she'd come fast, others she'd edge herself, begging for permission that I, nothing more than a witness, would never give.

Some nights I'd keep my distance. On others I'd circle the bed, or lean in to ghost her skin with the warmth of my breath. But I'd never touch her, and once she was done, I'd slip away and close the door without uttering a single word.

We never, ever talked about it, not in advance, or afterwards. She'd come find me cooking dinner and pretend she'd been napping, or in the shower. There's no thrill like keeping secrets from your own wife, when you know full well she knows what you've just done.

Fuck, she's brilliant.

It was Saskia's game, and she was in charge, but I knew, for her, the thrill was in thinking I could be anyone. I've often wondered what it would have been like to bring another man home with me. Would she be able to tell if we pulled two seats to the bedside? And how would she react knowing there were two sets of eyes on her, like there are right now?

I'm sure I could sit here with my mouth shut and watch the scene before me unfold, but I also love the idea of being in charge, even if I'm not involved in a physical sense.

"Do you know it was always my dream to watch her get fucked by another man?"

Saskia whimpers, her slender fingers clinging to the front of his top as they devour each other.

"Take off his shirt," I tell her. She shifts onto her knees, lifting it up and over his head. They pull apart for the briefest second before kissing harder.

"If you're going to fuck my wife, then I'm going to teach you how she likes to be pleasured."

Henry groans when Saskia drags her nails down his bare chest, hooking them inside the waistband of his pants. His hands dig into her hair and any nerves he might have previously had disappear as he loses himself to her touch.

She slips her hands inside, looping them around his waist to squeeze his ass.

"Uh-huh," I scold. "Get her naked first."

Henry hauls the blankets away, and they work together to strip her out of her top and bottoms.

She is as heavenly as ever, and I admire her wide hips, the fullness of her belly, breasts that hang heavy with need.

"I've never seen more perfect tits, have you, Henry?"

"No," he moans, breaking their kiss to look down and take both in his hands. He squeezes gently and Saskia's head tips back, her long hair tickling her spine.

"Her nipples are sensitive. You have to start soft and slow. Show me so I know you understand."

Henry dips his head to kiss the slope of her shoulder, out to the tip and then back along the collarbone. His thumbs roll over her nipples and though my view is obstructed, I know the feeling of them pebbling to stiff peaks well. Saskia's hands rake into his hair, pulling his mouth down as she arches up to meet him.

"Greedy girl," I tease. She twists her head and her eyes lock on mine, then roll back when he closes his lips around one nipple and sucks hard.

Oh, it is so fucking on.

Chapter 8

Henry

WHENEVER I'VE THOUGHT ABOUT getting my hands on Saskia again, I never once imagined her ex would be in the room with us. And yet, I'm more turned on than ever.

I might not know Saskia as intimately as Casper does, but there was no hiding the look in her eye when his suggestion sunk in.

The part of me that wanted him to leave evaporated the second I felt the heat of her tongue stroking against mine. All those years I've waited to do this again, I don't give a fuck if we have a witness. I only care about her.

Beneath the tip of my tongue, her nipple tightens, the other doing the same between my thumb and fingertip.

My cock is aching for her touch, but I could ignore it all night to focus on just this. Could spend hours tasting her, nipping the soft skin underneath her breasts between my teeth, sucking it until I leave marks.

My plan was to spend this week learning the landscape of her body. To go back to New York knowing how every part of her responds to my touch, my kisses.

Now all I want to do is close my eyes and focus on the shift in her breathing, see what parts of her elicit more of these pretty little moans. I want to make this a Christmas she'll never forget. The possibilities are endless.

"What do you want?" I ask her, but Casper answers before she can.

"Would you like to tell him, darling? Or shall I?"

"You tell him," she says, pulling away to lean back against the pillows. She drags me with her, and behind me he chuckles darkly. Normally, that would piss me off, but if Saskia is the prize in his game, I'm not complaining.

"You'll never be left wondering with this one, Henry. She'll always make it clear exactly what she wants."

She shifts to put one leg on either side of where I kneel before her, and with her hair spread across her pillows like golden silk, she really is a vision.

"Fuck her with your tongue," Casper says. "She needs a man who isn't afraid to get messy."

We didn't do this last time, and it's been my second biggest regret, after letting her go in the first place. That I had her naked in my bed and didn't get to taste her makes me feel like the biggest fool on earth. Especially when she was so good at using her mouth on me.

Cupping her ankle, I slide it up the bed, making her bend her knee and open wider for me. Her pussy is slick and pink, and though her body is older than the last time I saw her naked, she's more beautiful than ever.

Her hips are already squirming, and it's an unbelievable turn on to see her this needy. I could take my time, work her up to begging for it, but I've waited long enough for this taste of heaven.

One last glance to check she's OK with this confirms just how much she wants it too. Her eyes stayed locked with mine and I dip my head to sweep my tongue through her soaked folds.

Her chest heaves, fingers clutching at bedsheets when I circle her clit, nudging it side to side, watching, learning all the ways she likes to receive pleasure.

Behind me, Casper moans, but it's Saskia's I'm more interested in. The little whimpering sounds she makes when I swipe long, slow licks either side of her entrance. I can tell she's holding back, and I want her to truly let herself go with me.

My fingers slip inside her with ease, two at first, but I'll work her up to a third. I feel her tighten around me and my cock throbs, desperate to get in on the action.

I have always loved to give pleasure this way. To worship a woman with my mouth, to make her shake and writhe against me. If, like Casper says, she needs a man who isn't afraid to get messy, then I'm the only man she'll ever need.

Palming her thighs, I push them wide, opening her up so I can bury my tongue inside her. I savour the taste, the heady mix of salt and lust, years of wanting finally fulfilled.

Casper's fingers grip the hair at the back of my head, and I flinch, but only because I didn't expect it. He tightens his hold, working with me to move my head back and forth.

Saskia's thighs clamp tight around my head and he growls. "Hold her legs open so I can watch."

I pin one down while he pulls at the other, and bury my face in close.

"Show me your tongue," he says, pulling my hair. I don't know why taking instructions from this dickhead is turning me on so much, but I tip my head back, open my mouth, and push it out for him. He swipes one finger down the middle, scooping up the mix of my spit and her juices. Wide-eyed and slack-jawed, I watch as he brings it to his own mouth, wrapping his lips around it and sucking it clean.

"Delicious. Now suck her clit. Hard. That always turns her into a fucking puddle."

I don't take my eyes off of Saskia's as I drop my head a little lower, spit on her, then clamp my lips around that aching bundle of nerves. At the same time, I plunge my fingers back in, curling them up and stroking her from the inside.

She comes instantly, hips shooting off the bed so hard it's like a punch in the face. Casper helps me hold her still while she writhes, her orgasm flooding her system, her body convulsing, pretty moans filling the small room.

"Fuck me," she pleads, her head twisting from side to side, hands groping at her tits.

Casper opens the bedside drawer, and Saskia lets out a stroppy moan.

"You don't want a condom?" he asks her, and she shakes her head.

"Hmm," he says, tapping his lip. "When were you last tested, Henry?"

"Last year. All clear," I tell him, tilting her face towards mine. "I haven't been with anyone since then."

I was waiting for you.

Saskia smiles softly, nuzzling into my palm as I stroke her hair. She knows, because she was waiting too.

"She's had the all clear too," Casper says, and beneath me, her smile morphs into a frown.

"How do you know that?" she asks.

"I read your email," he shrugs. I make a mental note to put an end to that shit as soon as possible. "You had a wax yesterday, too, but Henry already knows that."

My gaze casts back down to where, beneath a neat strip of hair, she is smooth and glistening, and so fucking sexy.

"Wear a condom anyway," he says, shoving one into my palm. "It would be a cruel irony if the woman who doesn't want kids ends up pregnant the first time she sleeps with someone else."

There's much more for me and her to interrogate there, but it can wait. Tearing open the packet, I roll it on quickly while Saskia shifts into the middle of the bed.

"Lie down, Henry," Casper says. "I want to watch my wife ride you."

"Are you OK?" I ask her, ignoring him for a second. I never dreamed this is how our night would turn out, and I'm not complaining, but I'm only enjoying myself if she is.

"Yes," she nods, moving quickly up onto her knees. "I'm so good."

Saskia wastes no time guiding me inside her, her head thrown back as she sinks down inch by inch. My hands grip her hips, guiding her into position until the entire length of me is buried inside her.

Casper moves to stand at the side of the bed and shoves one hand into her hair, holding her in place so her eyes are on me. When he wraps his other hand around her slender throat, her eyes roll back and she grinds harder.

"This is what she likes," he says, as if I couldn't tell from the way her pussy is clenching around me. "No pressure, just possess her. Own her. Rule her body."

He licks a long, wet stripe from her jaw to her ear, and she tightens again.

"I told you it was always my dream to watch her fuck another man. Do you know her dream?"

I shake my head, and he releases her hair, stroking his hand down to one peaked nipple. I watch as he pinches and pulls until she squeals. He brings his cupped palm up to her mouth.

"Spit," he commands and Saskia obeys without flinching, a hot string of saliva catching on her chin.

Casper's hand disappears behind her, and with his fingers still at her throat, he lets her angle her body forward. Her eyes never leave mine, and when they widen, I can tell the exact moment his fingers work at her tight entrance.

"She dreams of being taken by two men at the same time," he says. My hands grip harder into her hips as she bucks in my lap, her breath shuddering at the moment he enters her.

I can feel it too, the extra pressure against my cock pushing from the other side of her walls. It's fucking intense. I've never felt anything like it. Never *done* anything like this.

"This is her dream. Well, a taste of it," he laughs. "I bet you want more, don't you, angel? That's it. Fuck up into her. She likes that a lot."

Saskia is boneless while I pound her, garbled sounds pouring from her mouth, hands scrambling to grasp at my chest, my arms, the sheets, anything. She shifts her feet flat on the bed so she's better supported, and I reach underneath her to help lift her up and drop her back down, over and over and over.

The hairs on Casper's arm tickle against mine, his warm skin throwing another sensation into the mix.

Saskia's knees knock together, her thighs trembling as her orgasms roars forth. White heat floods through me when she clenches so hard I fall straight off the cliff-edge with her.

"Good girl, good girl," Casper whispers, nuzzling the side of her head with his face until she flops onto my chest.

Casper pulls his hands away and crouches by her side, tipping his head to watch her ride out her orgasm. "Look at her. Drunk on your cock. She's such a good little plaything, isn't she?"

The last of my release is still filling the condom when he stands and heads for the door.

"Where are you going?" I ask. "I thought you were going to—"

The weight of disappointment shocks me.

Did I even want that?

"Sometimes it's good to give her what she wants. Sometimes it's better to make her wait until she least expects it. You'll soon learn. Sleep well, my friend."

Saskia is still panting, trembling in my arms as the door snicks closed. I stroke my hands up and down her back until she looks up, resting her chin on my chest.

"Are you OK, darling?" I ask, sweeping the damp hair away from her face.

"What the fuck just happened?" Panic flares in her eyes as what we just experienced together truly sinks in.

Sitting up against the headboard, I lift her with me, and she curls into my chest. Her head fits into the crook of my neck like a piece of a puzzle that's been just out of reach for as long as I've known her. There is so much to say, but I'm bone tired. From travelling, from jet-lag, from emptying inside her after the best fuck of my life. I can't even begin to process it, let alone explain it to her.

"I have no idea, but I think we should get cleaned up and sleep. We'll talk about it in the morning."

Chapter 9

Saskia

THERE IS A SOFT, warm dent next to me in bed when I finally wake up. The room is dark, and when I reach for the small clock on the bedside table, I'm pleasantly surprised to see it's after 9am. Thank God for thick curtains and quiet countryside.

I haven't slept this long in forever, and though parts of my body are physically aching, there's an inner peace I haven't felt for some time.

I slept with Henry.

More than that. I fell asleep in his arms after an expertly delivered orgasm, just like I've always dreamed of.

Oh, and my ex-husband happened to be there too. That part I never saw coming.

Yes, it's always been my fantasy to sleep with two men, to have two pairs of hands on me, two mouths focused solely on my pleasure. Two cocks inside me at the same time, if I was feeling really fucking bold.

Last night was the closest I've come to that experience, and though it was not the way I imagined sleeping with Henry again, I can't pretend I didn't love every minute.

Even with Casper there directing our every move, it was Henry's hands all over me, Henry filling me, Henry's eyes never leaving mine.

Until Casper got handsy too.

My lips press together and my belly tightens at the memory of his hand in my hair, stroking my spine, pressing into me while I ground my hips into Henry. The sensation was phenomenal.

Casper and I have had plenty of sex while I've worn a plug, or when he's taken me from behind and used a toy at the same time, but none of that came close to the simultaneous pleasure brought on by Henry's cock and Casper's fingers.

Exhausted as I am, it's now all I can think about. I want more, and waking up alone feels cruel when I know they're both nearby. Unless Casper has already left, as promised. That certainly would be an odd goodbye.

Trust him to turn up and fuck with my head just when I was starting to get a little clarity on my future.

I yank a pillow over my face, scream into it, then force myself to get up and throw on my robe.

The low murmur of voices and the scent of fresh coffee drift in when I open the bedroom door. He's still here. In my house. With my new... boyfriend? At least they're not arguing.

Hovering at the top of the stairs, I lean over the bannister to hear them more clearly over the crackle of the fire they've already lit.

"She always had a thing for you, you know. And you have my blessing," I hear Casper say. "I told her the same before you joined us last night."

"I appreciate that," Henry says, his voice even and calm. I breathe a sigh of relief, knowing there's no animosity between them. Breakfast will already be awkward enough.

"I know you will take care of her, treat her well, give her everything I could not. But while we're stuck here," Casper continues. "I think we might as well have some fun together, if that's what you want?"

The tips of my ears burn the same way they do when you realise someone is talking about you, but this time, the rest of my body burns with it.

"If that's what *she* wants," Henry says firmly. "Saskia's in charge here. At all times. Not me, and not you. I think we all enjoyed ourselves last night, but she calls the shots from now on."

I pinch my lips together and enjoy the sensation of knowing that Henry is in my corner. But wait...

Stuck here? What is he talking about?

Casper promised he'd leave first thing this morning.

On the upstairs landing, I peel back the hallway curtain and gasp at the view across the fields. A blanket of thick snow covers everything as far as the eye can see.

I bolt down the stairs two at a time, throwing open the front door for a view in the opposite direction. All three of our cars are buried under at least a foot of snow, and thanks to drifts, the road beyond is barely visible.

"Good morning, Saskia."

"Good morning, my angel."

I turn to find both men behind me, cradling steaming cups of fresh coffee. My skin pricks and a shiver rolls down my spine, but I couldn't say whether it's from the brisk winter air or the sight before me.

Henry is topless in grey marl sweatpants, leaning casually against the back of the sofa with his legs crossed at the ankle. Over at the dining table, Casper is also half dressed in a similar pair of sweatpants, and I feel like I've walked into the men's locker room at the gym. He sits with his chin in his palm, arm propped on his elbow. It makes me wonder who got half naked first.

"How did you sleep?" Casper asks, his eyes raking down my body and back up again. He's slipped his hands beneath this robe many times, and from the subtle tick of his jaw, I can tell he's thinking about it.

I close the door behind me and pull my robe tighter. "You're supposed to be leaving after breakfast."

He raises his eyebrows. "Impossible, it seems, but we can still have those pancakes you promised me."

All my plans for a relaxing few days with my new man unravel as I find myself in an unfortunate position, standing between them.

I need Casper to leave. Need space to think, to breathe. This room is stifling with the heat from the fire, their two large frames taking up all the space around me.

"Stop thinking so much," Henry says, moving to my side and wrapping an arm around my waist. I soften naturally into him, my fingertips curling around the tight muscles of his stomach. It's bold of him to touch me in front of the man I married, but after last night, there's no denying we're more than friends. "He can stay. There's plenty of room, and we'll figure it out."

"I don't have enough food for us all," I object, my mind already scrambling to adjust the recipes I have planned to cook for three servings instead of two. They've set the table with fruit and oven-fresh pastries, but I know these men have big appetites, and after last night, I'm ravenous myself.

"Please," Casper laughs. "I have met you. Even when you're cooking for two, you have enough for ten."

"That's true," Henry laughs, pressing a kiss to my temple. "You take a seat, and I'll make you a coffee."

Chapter 10

Saskia

I SIT DOWN OPPOSITE Casper and try my hardest not to look at the body I've spent so many years admiring. When his art isn't going well, he fights his demons in the gym, and if his current physique is anything to go by, something is troubling him lately.

"Are you well, wife?" he asks, leaning in and lowering his voice. "Sore?"

"Stop that," I hiss. "And enough of the wife shit. What are you doing?"

"I have something for you," he says, producing a wrapped box from the chair next to him.

I tear off the paper to find a new jigsaw puzzle, a 1000 piece picture of an Italian villa. The cheeky bastard. I narrow my eyes at him. "Thought you didn't know I'd be here?"

"I was planning to leave it here for when you next visited," he shrugs. "But now we can do it together, just like old times."

Old times where we'd spend hours around this table fitting pieces together, pausing only for snacks or to get naked in front of the fireplace. Heat creeps up my spine at the memory, and I look away in case my expression gives me away.

"Here you go." Henry sets a cup of coffee down in front of me, then rests his hand on the back of my chair. His thumb strokes a line up the middle of my back and I lean into it. "Oat milk and half a spoonful of brown sugar, right?"

"Right," I nod, looking up at him. The hard planes of his chest, the scruff of his stubble, those full lips I want to spend the day kissing.

This is what I wanted this week. The two of us slipping into easy companionship, taking care of each other, touching each other freely, looking without guilt.

Casper leans back in his chair, crosses his arms, and huffs loudly. "I know how she takes her coffee, Henry. I have been married to her for years. You have nothing to prove."

Henry takes the seat next to me. Spreading his legs wide, he pats his thigh and I barely think of the implications of our company when I hop into his lap.

"You must be starving after last night," he says, wrapping one arm tightly around my waist. He sweeps my hair away from my neck and presses a soft kiss there. "I know I am."

I've never seen this side of him before. Competitive, arrogant, entitled. I deal with those sorts of people every day of my life, both artists and buyers. I can't say it's normally a turn on, but watching Henry tap into his possessive side is definitely doing it for me. As is the warmth of his thigh radiating through the layers of fabric between us.

His allure is in his quiet confidence. At six foot three, he commands a room simply by being in it, but his quiet charm makes everyone else feel like the most important person there. He listens, never interrupts, and when he speaks, he chooses every word carefully.

It's been a while since I've seen him work, but I know he seals deals with a smile and the raise of one eyebrow. Though he's made a name for himself in the New York art world, I know for sure he doesn't have to work half as hard as I do. People flock to him not just for the association with his name, but because his company makes their day.

His client list rivals mine in size and status, but he's never been my competition, always a cheerleader.

It's no wonder I'm putty in his hands as he boosts me up, twisting me so my legs drape over his other thigh. The silk of my robe slips slightly, revealing a swathe of skin above my knee that he warms with his palm.

I sip my coffee, peering over the rim at Casper watching the blatant display of possession in front of him. Henry reaches for a bowl of grapes, plucking a ripe one from the stem and offering it up to my mouth. I open for him, letting my tongue sneak just past my lips to catch the tip of his finger.

The room is silent but for the roar of the fire, and it may as well be raging inside me. The combination of Henry's hands and Casper's eyes on me is deadly, and my mind is flashing between thoughts of last night and what more could happen between the three of us.

"What would you like to do today, darling?" Henry asks casually, and my core tightens. What I really want is more sex, and lots of it, but I'm not quite bold enough to ask outright.

Casper and I have discussed my threesome fantasies plenty in the past. Sometimes while basking in the afterglow, or on nights we whispered our dirty wishes into each other's ears in busy bars.

We've discussed, at length, the where, the what, and the how, but never considered *when* it might happen or *who* it would be with.

My conversations with Henry these past few months have been another story entirely. Yes, there's been plenty of flirting, but I got the impression he wanted to wait until we were together in person to talk about sex, and I followed his lead.

We've now slept together twice, almost two decades apart, and those experiences couldn't have been more different. I'd imagined we'd take our time to understand each other's needs, not jump straight in with a threesome, but then I remember the conversation I overheard earlier.

'Saskia's in charge.'

'She calls the shots.'

Casper said as much when we were alone in my room.

'I want to fulfil her every last fantasy.'

But surely last night was a one-off? And I wouldn't want to risk whatever is unfolding with Henry by confessing any lingering desires for more sex with my ex-husband.

"Casper bought me a puzzle," is what I finally manage to squeak out.

Henry says, planting a trail of kisses along my shoulder. "Sounds like the perfect way to unwind."

Casper's eyes drift down and to the right, locked on Henry's movements. When Henry slips his hand inside my robe, cupping my breast in his warm hand, Casper growls—*actually fucking growls*—at the sight.

"What's wrong, Casper?" Henry laughs behind my ear, and my eyes flutter closed. "Feeling left out?"

"Don't fuck with me, you bastard," Casper snaps. "She's still my wife on paper."

His words drag me out of my lust-filled trance, replacing my heightened sensitivity with frustration. I thought we'd cleared the air last night. Technically, in the eyes of the law, I'm still his wife, but he knows full well my heart is no longer his, and my body has always been my own, no matter how much I've loved submitting to him in the past.

Henry's hand slips between my legs, nudging them apart a little, and that pisses me off too. I want him to touch me because he wants to, not to win some dick-swinging contest.

I yank his hand away and push out of his grasp. "That's enough. We may be stuck here, but I won't have my Christmas ruined with fighting. Do you understand me?"

Their backs stiffen and they both nod, clearly not used to being told what to do.

"And put some shirts on," I add, waving my hands at their bare chests. "This is ridiculous."

I snatch a *pain au chocolat* from the table and take my coffee over to the sofa, leaving them both to think about what they've done, and me to think about what I'll do next.

Chapter 11

Saskia

THE MORNING PASSES WITHOUT further drama. After changing into cream cashmere loungewear, I curl up on the sofa and lose myself in a book I've been meaning to read for months. Casper appears now and then, with hot chocolate or warm cookies, and Henry tugs my feet into his lap for a foot rub. A girl could get used to this, each of them making it up to me in their own way.

The three of us revolve around each other like this is all perfectly normal. I make a simple country vegetable soup for lunch and serve it with warm bread and butter laced with salt crystals.

The boys behave impeccably while we eat, talking about work and their various mutual friends on the art scene whilst both keeping their hands to themselves. It's strangely reminiscent of meals Casper and I have shared with Henry over the years, on his visits to London, or when we've spent a long weekend in New York.

Though Henry has always been my friend first, he and Casper have gotten on well over the years. This morning was the first glimpse of rivalry I've seen between them, but, thankfully, all seems to be forgotten now.

After lunch, Henry runs me a bath, and I enjoy a long soak in the tub. The bathroom was the first thing I upgraded when I bought the cottage, knowing how much I'd enjoy relaxing here after a busy week in the city.

It's a small space, but my architect worked some magic to fit both a roll-top bath and a walk-in shower. The thin window allows little light in, but the brass wall-sconces give the room a luxurious feel, as do the expensive products I keep here year-round.

Downstairs, I find the boys watching a Christmas film. I snuggle into Henry's lap and he covers me with one of the many throw blankets I keep scattered around the living room. In no time at all, I doze off, my exhausted body and overworked brain taking the rest I desperately crave, in the arms of the man I adore.

When I wake up alone, I find Henry has settled me against a pillow and covered me with a blanket. I stretch out, rolling my neck from side to side. The low winter sun gleams through the window, lights twinkle softly on the tree, and I hear Henry humming a Christmas song in the kitchen.

Winter nights in the cottage feel like being in a world of your own. It's already fairly secluded, exactly what I wanted from a country getaway, but with the addition of snow, we're truly blanketed from the outside world. I turned my phone off when Henry arrived, determined to fully disconnect from work, from life, and from the shadow of my separation.

Our lawyers have handled everything, and though there hasn't been any drama along the way, knowing we still need to sign those final papers is a weight I can't wait to lift. Of all the contracts and deals I've signed in my life, this will be the least enjoyable, but I assumed come

January all would be done. Not that I'd be sharing a house with him again for Christmas.

"There's my beautiful girl," Henry says, appearing at my side with a glass of chilled Champagne. "You sleep well?"

"Very." I smile and take a sip, enjoying the sensation as bubbles flood my tongue. He takes a seat by my feet, lifting them into his lap once more. The man can't stop touching me, and I'm not complaining.

With no sign of Casper, I catch a hint of the time I thought we'd be spending alone together, and it's everything I've dreamed of. Still, in a cottage of this size, he can't be far, and I know I won't have much time to talk to Henry before being interrupted.

"Are you OK?" I ask, reaching for his hand and curling both of mine around it. His other hand slips between my calves, thumb pressing into the tight muscles there.

"I'm wonderful, darling."

"Are you really, though? This is..."

My eyes dart towards the stairs. Fucking crazy is what it is, and talking about it with Henry has me feeling shy, something I never felt with Casper.

"I don't know what this is. Last night was fun, but it was a lot of pressure to put on you without us having a conversation first."

"Last night," he whispers, leaning closer to conspire with me. "Did you enjoy yourself?"

"Yes," I sign, moaning softly when his fingers coast past my knee on their journey north. My breath quickens. "Very much."

"What did you enjoy about it?"

I don't even have to think of an answer. The two of them working me to orgasm scratched a deep itch I'd never have been able to reach alone. The release was phenomenal, and I slept better than I have in years. My body tingles at the memory of Henry's hands and Casper's words.

"You controlled my body, he controlled my mind. I didn't have to do anything but enjoy it."

His fingers tease the hem of my shorts, slipping up underneath and pinching the sensitive skin on the inside of my thigh. "You like giving up control?"

He pinches me higher, and all I can do is nod. I can't speak, can't look away, can't do anything while his touch pulls me under his hypnotic spell.

"You'd do it again?"

"Yes," I moan softly.

"And more?"

Casper bounds down the stairs before I can answer, with a large black box in his hands. "Look! I found our box of treasures."

Chapter 12

Henry

SASKIA AND I JUMP apart at the interruption, even though there was nothing to interrupt.

Yet.

She twists her head to look over the back of the sofa, cheeks turning pink. I'm no mind reader, but from the look on Casper's face, I have a pretty good idea of what this *'box of treasures'* might contain.

She ignores him and reaches for her book, so I grab a pen from the coffee table and return to yesterday's newspaper. Our ignorance only spurs Casper on.

"I think I'll charge these," he says, rummaging in the box, then leaning over the sofa cushions to wave a fairly heavy-duty wand in Saskia's face. "Then later we can show Henry how they all work."

"I know my way around a vibrator, mate," I tell him without looking up from my crossword.

At the other end of the sofa, Saskia gasps, then frowns, and I detect a hint of jealousy. There's nothing to be jealous of. The past is the past, and though there've been women along the way, I'm hoping she'll be my first and last.

Our first time was a pact, two friends giving each other the gift of their virginity without the pressure of throwing it away on someone we didn't really care about. We both felt confident we'd be able to look each other in the eye the next day without it being awkward. True to our word, we never spoke about it again. Until last night.

I wouldn't change that experience for the world, but it was the opposite end of the spectrum to the sex I've grown to crave since then. We may barely know each other in this department, but I've dated a fair bit in New York, and I'm no novice when it comes to the multitude of ways to bring a woman to orgasm.

Saskia and I have talked about plenty in our years of friendship, but our sex lives have always been fairly off-limits. I had no interest in hearing about what she was getting up to with her husband, and telling her about my exploits in New York felt inappropriate when we'd both agreed we were best as friends.

After last night, though, there's clearly more to Saskia, more to both of them, than meets the eye. And that's great news for me. I've had no doubts about my longing to pursue something with her, but having a partner whose tastes and desires match yours is definitely a bonus.

Knowing Saskia, she's probably had the same worry herself. Would she be going from a partner like Casper to someone more vanilla? Hopefully, she has her answer.

When I heard him moving around the cottage this morning, I wasn't sure how to approach the situation. After going round in circles, I slipped out of Saskia's bed and found him in the kitchen. There was none of the awkwardness you might expect after sleeping with a man's wife in front of him. Casper even shook my hand and thanked me, for goodness' sake.

Last night took me by surprise, but it all felt natural in the confines of her bedroom. Being trapped by heavy snowfall isn't going to help us avoid talking about it, but if they're not freaking out, then I don't see the need to either. All that matters to me is her happiness, and from the way he spoke about hoping to fulfil her wishes, it seems like that's what matters to Casper, too.

Sure, we could wait out the snowstorm with jigsaw puzzles and crosswords, but if there's a box of sex toys on the table, I know which games I'd rather play.

Chapter 13
Saskia

I KNOW FOR A fact the box in Casper's hands is full of things Henry and I are nowhere near exploring together. This week was supposed to be about us having a fresh start, not fucking in front of my ex and passing the time using the thousands of pounds worth of sex toys we kept here.

That couldn't be further from the experiences Henry and I have previously shared. That night, all those years ago, was everything a woman could want for her first time. Slow, safe, romantic even. He tidied his college dorm room, lit candles, and picked music. He dressed up a little and was so handsome, even though he was still figuring out who he was. We both were back then.

We've obviously got a stronger sense of ourselves now, and of our sexual needs.

"Ah, there you are, my old friends," Casper says, faking a double-cheek kiss on what, from the corner of my eye, appears to be a pair of nipple clamps. "I've missed you."

Henry and I steal glances at each other, trying not to laugh as we continue to ignore Casper's teasing.

"Ooh, handcuffs," he says, spinning them around one finger. "We've had a lot of fun with these, haven't we, angel?"

Henry's eyes flare, and I can't tell if he's picturing himself using them with me, or me using them with Casper.

"Maybe we should handcuff our guest and make him watch us fuck," Casper laughs, tossing them back into the box.

My gaze glances down to where Henry's cock visibly twitches beneath his sweatpants, and suddenly a little cuff-play is all I can think about. Except, under these circumstances, it's not *him* I'd want to restrain.

Casper and I talked often about playing with other people but never followed through on our fantasies. My taste for exhibitionism has only ever gone as far as him watching me. We always liked the idea of him seeing me with another man, and he orchestrated that with perfection last night.

Even if he didn't quite give me everything I was hoping for, Casper clearly came here with an agenda, and he's not getting to play on his terms twice.

I down my Champagne and get up from the sofa, snatching the box from Casper's hands and dropping it onto the dining table.

I pull a chair into the middle of the room and point at it. "Sit down."

"Oooh, I love it when she gets bossy," he says to Henry, rubbing his palms together.

"Now," I snap.

He takes a seat and pats his thigh expectantly. I ignore him and root in the box until I find what I'm looking for. A pair of black handcuffs that have been well used over the years.

"Hands behind you," I tell him. He reaches back, presenting his thick wrists to me. Bending, I fasten them together, not too tightly, but enough that he won't be able to escape.

Casper was the more naturally dominant partner during our time together, with a knack for honing in on the exact things that would tip me over the edge. Occasionally he'd lean into a more submissive role, but it was never long before he'd put me back in my place.

Tomorrow the snow will melt, and he'll head back to London. This might be the perfect way to end things, on a high, with me in the driving seat.

"I've had enough of your shit," I bark at him, and he twists his head to look at me. "You thought you could come here and act like you're in charge? You don't have that power over me anymore, Casper."

"I'll give you all the power, baby. Any time you like," he teases.

Grabbing Henry's hand, I pull him up from the sofa and lead him through to the kitchen for a private word.

"Where are you going?" Casper yells. "Don't leave me here like this."

He rattles a little in the chair, but I know it's all for show. He'll be rattling more in a few minutes. I poke my head around the corner and throw him my sweetest smile. "We'll be right back."

"What are you up to, naughty girl?" Henry says, hauling me back into the kitchen and out of Casper's sight.

"I want to get him back for what he put us through last night," I whisper. "Are you game?"

A look of panic flashes across his face. "I thought you said you enjoyed last night?"

"I did," I say, sliding my hands up his chest until they settle on his shoulders. His skin is so warm, I want to jump up and wrap my legs around his waist. "I promise I did, but I don't like him lording it over us. He knew we would be here."

"What? How?"

"He brought me a gift. And he gave himself away when he mentioned my test results last night. I forgot he has access to my email and my calendar. He would have been able to see my appointments, your flight times."

"Our messages?"

He looks shocked, and though there's been nothing explicit between us, it thrills me to know he thinks our recent exchanges are scandal worthy.

I suppose they would be, if I were a happily married woman with a husband sleeping by her side, but that hasn't been my reality for a while now. Our messages have always been vaguely overfamiliar, but recently we've been more direct in our flirting.

I cup his face and shake my head. "No, he doesn't have access to those. Though he clearly had some idea of what was about to happen between us."

"Because we're inevitable, right?" His arms wrap around my waist, tugging me against him, and my heart soars. *'Inevitable'* is how I've been thinking of him, too.

"We are. So I think it's about time I showed him he's not the boss of me anymore."

"What did you have in mind?"

I bite my lip and consider my words before deciding that telling him might spoil the fun for all of us. "Do you trust me?"

"Of course, completely."

"You'll tell me if I push it too far?"

His eyes flare and the corner of his mouth lifts into a devious smile. "What are you planning, you little minx?"

"We haven't got time to talk, Henry. Are you willing to let me take control?" I tip my head up, ghosting my lips over his as I cup him between the legs. I feel his cock, already hard beneath his sweatpants, twitch against my wrist. "I'll take that as a yes."

Chapter 14
Saskia

BACK IN THE LIVING room, I set another chair behind Casper, facing the opposite direction.

"What is going on, angel?"

"Sit down, Henry." A power high surges through me when he does as he's told. "Hands behind your back too."

With a smile on his face, he presents them in the same way. I crouch to fasten his cuffs between the two chairs, looping them through Casper's so their arms are connected.

"What the fuck is this?" Casper grunts when he discovers I've chained them to each other. Henry's smile morphs into a scowl and I wonder if he might be rethinking this.

I dart upstairs, tugging off my clothes as I go. There's a lot of underwear in my drawer, and I slip into new black lingerie before covering myself up with a silky robe.

Back downstairs, there's one more thing I need from the box of treasures before my plan can really begin. I make a big show of sauntering past them and bending over in front of Casper while I take my time looking for it.

It's surprisingly fun taunting him like this. Casper has only ever liked being told what to do when ultimately he's still in control. Considering how much I enjoyed relinquishing control in the bedroom, we were a perfect fit in that sense. Though judging by the wet spot I can already feel in my underwear, I might enjoy being the one in control more than I thought.

He makes all sorts of approving noises when I bend further, fully aware that my robe is riding high, but not quite high enough for him to see underneath. Finally, I find what I'm looking for, just as I feel the hem of my robe being lifted. When I look over my shoulder, Casper is wearing a shit-eating grin, with one leg stretching out to nudge it up with his foot.

I round on him fast, gripping his jaw firmly. "Do that again and I'll cuff your legs, too."

His eyes are wild, the pulse in his neck visibly thumping. Looming over him, I rub my chest against his face before tying a black blindfold over his eyes. He's like a dog, growling, snapping his teeth against my skin, but I'm not afraid of his bite. I might be a little afraid of the consequences of what I'm about to put him through, though.

Once I'm satisfied he can't see anything, I squeeze the bulge in his pants hard. He whimpers, then groans when I release him, moving behind him to focus on Henry.

"Henry," Casper says, his head thrashing as he tries to regain his vision. "Are you blindfolded?"

"No," Henry answers, his chest rising and falling fast. "You blind-folded him? What's going on?"

Loosening the belt, I let my robe drop to the floor and bend at the waist to rest my palms flat on Henry's strong thighs. "He likes to watch, but let's see how much he likes to listen."

My tongue sweeps along Henry's bottom lip, and he tips his head back, opening for me to kiss him deeply. Any plans to drag this out fall by the wayside when I climb into his lap, straddling him with my knees gripping his hips. My dining table chairs are made of solid oak, but they were designed for dining, not for two people fucking on them.

Henry's erection is solid beneath me, and my hips roll instinctively while my hands cup his face and keep his mouth on mine.

"Take my dick out," he moans, his own hips flexing up against me.

I lean back, arching my tits up towards his face. "Excuse me?"

"Take my dick out... please?"

"I didn't say you could speak," I tell him sternly, covering his mouth with my palm. "Don't be so impatient. You'll get what's coming to you when I'm good and ready."

I kiss him again, this time letting him take the lead. His tongue sweeps softly over mine, then firmly as he picks up the pace. His soft moans get deeper when I hitch myself higher into his lap. My nails dig into his shoulders, gripping him through his t-shirt and steadying myself. His kisses are dizzying and it would be easy to topple backwards while he's unable to hold me in place.

"Tell me what you see," Casper begs behind him, and Henry and I stop kissing, both holding back a laugh as I keep rocking my hips against him. Our silence drives Casper wild. "Fucking tell me what you see."

Henry looks up at me with pleading eyes, and I can tell he wants to brag about what he has that Casper doesn't.

"She's in my lap, grinding into me."

"Is she naked?"

"No. She took her robe off, but her underwear is still on."

"Lace?" Casper asks, and Henry mumbles his answer while I stroke my chest with my hands, pushing my breasts together. "Fuck. Bite her nipples through the fabric. She loves the way that feels."

Henry lifts one eyebrow as if to ask for clarification and I nod, cupping one breast and bringing it up to his mouth.

He spits on it and laps eagerly, smearing the wetness around my nipple, then blowing through the damp lace. The feeling is incredible, as is the rake of his teeth as he tugs it into his mouth. I feel the solid length of him throbbing against my soaked panties, jerking harder when he takes my other breast in his mouth and sucks long enough to mark me.

"Take it off, please?" he begs, and who am I to object? He's not the man I want to punish here. I reach behind me, and it's on the floor in seconds.

"What now?" Casper pleads, his cuffs rattling between them, but Henry's eager mouth is too busy licking and nibbling to answer. "Is her clit swollen? It gets so swollen when she's about to orgasm."

I almost laugh, but until he said it, I hadn't noticed how close I actually am. Apparently, he's listening closely after all.

Henry looks down between us, and I tug my underwear to one side, dig the nails on my other hand into his shoulders, and lean back so he can see. "Yeah, she's swollen. Fucking soaked, too."

All my grinding has left a dark patch on his grey sweatpants, and that turns me on even more.

"I knew she would be," Casper laughs. "I am the master of that pussy."

"Not anymore, you're not." Henry leans forward, his mouth capturing mine in a brutal kiss that nearly sends me over the edge.

His teeth sink into my lip, holding me there, and I briefly regret tying his hands up because my body knows instinctively how hard he'd grip hold of me if he could. If he had his way, I'm sure Henry would have his pants down and his cock buried inside me in seconds.

"You think you can make her come as hard as I do?" Casper shouts, and I slow my pace. I definitely don't want to come just yet.

"He's very noisy, isn't he?" I say to Henry. "Is he distracting you?"

"A little," he nods, his conspiratorial smirk goading me on.

"I find that unacceptable." I lace my words with condescension and lean in to speak close to both of their ears. "I don't want *anything* to distract me from the feeling of your cock filling me up. Why should I suffer just because he isn't good at sharing his toys?"

I lift myself off of Henry and let my underwear shift back into place. I have to bite my lip when I look down, his sweatpants straining where his cock tries to break free.

Henry groans loudly and behind him, Casper jerks in his seat. "What is she doing? What's happening?"

I saunter round to stand in front of Casper. He sniffs the air, listening eagerly for clues as to what's coming next, but I face away from him and bend over.

Slowly, I peel my underwear off, dragging them down my legs, wiggling my hips as I step out of them. It turns me on more than it should to torment him even while he can't see anything.

Years ago, I blindfolded him in the bed upstairs, hopped up on top of him, and used the vibrating wand mere inches from his face. He was as feral then as he is now, but that was his idea, and he holds none of the power here.

Gripping his hair, I tug his head back and drop a soft kiss on the tip of his nose.

"Open your mouth and stick your tongue out for me," I whisper.

He does as he's told, and I wonder what he thinks he's going to get a taste of. My tongue? A nipple? Judging by the way he thrashes from side to side, he certainly wasn't expecting me to ball up my soaked underwear and shove them inside.

I lick a hot, wet stripe from his mouth to his ear, the same way he did to me last night. "Now be a good boy and let me fuck my man in peace."

Chapter 15

Saskia

IN HINDSIGHT, I PROBABLY should have made Henry strip off before I handcuffed him to my ex-husband.

His tight-fitting t-shirt will have to stay on, but I manage to wiggle his trousers down over his hips and I'm delighted to find he's naked underneath.

Ignoring Casper's muffled frustrations, I pull them free, and toss them aside.

Henry's eyes widen when I climb back into his lap, sliding myself back and forth along the thick length of his shaft. The swollen head nudges against my clit and the pressure is so perfect, I know I could come from just this.

Still, I need more.

"You are not allowed to come inside me. Do you understand?"

He's not allowed to come inside me, because I have other plans for it.

"I understand," he nods.

"Good boy. I'm going to make myself come all over you, and you're going to tell me if you get too close."

When I lift up, his cock jerks upwards and sitting down on it feels like slipping into a warm bath. He's the perfect size. Not so big it's too much to handle, but enough to give me the stretch I've been so desperately craving.

There'll be time for hard, frantic fucking later, I'm sure. Casper is probably formulating a payback plan at this very moment. For now, all I want is to come, and come hard.

"Open," I tell Henry, slipping my fingers into his mouth to get them even wetter.

Locking my ankles around the legs of the chair, I wrap one arm around his shoulders and begin to work my clit in soft, sweeping circles. I really am swollen and aching, and despite his confinement, Henry still manages to thrust up into me, driving me even closer to the edge.

Our foreheads press together, eyes locked as white heat pools quickly in the pit of my stomach, then floods through the tops of my thighs. My fingers work faster, circles getting smaller and firmer as he whispers words of encouragement.

"I can feel that, you know?" I almost can't hear him over the sound of Casper bitching and moaning through his gag, but Henry nudges my head to one side to get his mouth closer to my ear. "Your perfect pussy is gripping me so fucking tight. You've never looked hotter than you do right now. I want you to soak me."

Their cuffs rattle, and I release my grip on Henry's shoulder, reach further back, and cover Casper's mouth with my palm. Pretending to ignore him is fun, but he is a part of this, too, and I don't want him to be completely left out.

His head tips back against Henry's shoulder, and he softens, pressing kisses to my skin. Combined with Henry bucking up into me, it's enough to push me right to the brink. A few firm strokes and I'm gone, every muscle in my body convulsing as I ride out my orgasm in Henry's lap.

"Holy fuck, Sass," he moans. "You need to get off me."

My legs are too shaky to stand, so I drop to my knees in front of him, my jaw hanging open at the sight of him jutting skyward, glistening from where I've drenched him. His cock looks angry and fit to burst, which makes me think I hopped off just in time.

This position always makes me feel submissive, but with him tied up, I have no option but to take control.

I spread my palms on the inside of his knees, pushing them out to the side so I can shuffle closer and lap up the mess I've made. I suck his balls into my mouth, then clean his length with my tongue, never looking away from his wide lust-filled eyes.

"Jesus Christ, who the fuck are you?" he says when I suck the tip between my lips, then push all the way down, nudging him against the back of my throat.

I like that a lot, the ecstasy spread across his face, the light sheen of sweat that coats his body, all lit up under the glow of the Christmas tree lights.

Casper has spent years encouraging me to tap into my sexual desires, and I can't wait to explore those depths with Henry. He's only just beginning to understand how good things can be between us.

Pulling back, I spit on his head and work it up and down with my fist while the other hand cups his balls, rolling and squeezing and gently tugging on them. Henry's breath turns choppy, his eyes glazing over and I think scrambling this man's brain might be my new hobby.

"Tell Casper what his whore wife is doing."

I tilt my head to run my tongue all the way along one side, licking from the base to the tip and back down again while Casper stamps his feet like a child who's had his toys taken away.

"Blow job," Henry pants. "Really good one. Sucking the soul—"

I make an indecent show of swirling my tongue around the tip and sucking hard while jerking his shaft in smooth, rhythmic motions.

"Oh, fuck, Sass. That's too good. I'm gonna—"

Henry's chair wobbles from side to side, their cuffs rattling between them. I dig my nails into his thighs and briefly panic that he might wrench one of Casper's arms out of its socket. The thought disappears when his body stiffens and I feel his hot, salty release fill my mouth.

I bob my head lower, wanting to make sure I get every last drop.

"Show me," Henry pleads, and I open my mouth for him to see where it's pooled on my tongue and filled the space beneath it. "Let me see you swallow it."

I'm about to, when Casper moans desperately, and I have a feeling he'd rather like to see me with a mouth full of cum, too. Even more so when it's not his own. The thought has my pussy throbbing all over again.

Closing my mouth, I shake my head slowly, rising to my feet and rounding the chairs. Yanking the blindfold off of Casper, I drop it on the floor and kneel before him.

He blinks rapidly, then lets out a keening sound as if it pains him to see me like this, stripped bare with a dark hickey rapidly blooming where Henry has sucked hard into the flesh of my breast.

It wasn't supposed to be like this. My plan was always to cuff him and blindfold him, to tease him up close to the action without being able to see what he was missing out on, but I can't help myself. The darkest part of me *wants* him to see me like this. Wants him to see that another man has touched me, and that I've loved every second of it.

With my hands on his knees, I push them wide and scoot closer, just like I did with Henry. Except instead of freeing him from his sweats, I throw my head back until the ends of my hair graze the base of my spine.

Opening wide, I show him the load Henry just blew in my mouth, and he whimpers around his gag, rattling in the chair as if this time he'll manage to break free.

I've spent so long aiming to please him that I briefly wonder what he wants me to do next, but I can't ask with my mouth full, even if I wanted to. This is not about him anymore, so instead I do what I want and push my tongue to the edge of my lip, forcing it to spill over the edge.

Casper watches intently as it trickles down my chin, rivulets finding the path of least resistance and dripping down to my neck. I adjust the angle of my body so it carries down to my tits, gradually pushing more from my mouth.

Over Casper's shoulder, Henry twists his head from side to side, desperate to see what he's missing out on, and I pocket that power too. He may have been the one to fuck me, but this next part is a little treat for my ex-husband's eyes only.

I shuffle back a little until there's space for me to spread my legs wider, while Henry's cum keeps dripping from my lips. Casper tracks it as it runs through the channel between my breasts, down over my stomach. Some of it pools in my bellybutton, the rest soaking into the trimmed strip of hair beneath.

He looks disappointed, but I have a secret. There's more where that came from.

Finally, I spit the last of Henry's cum into my hand and, using the other one to prop myself up, I lift my hips as high as they'll go. Wiggling my fingers, I let the creamy fluid drip onto my pink, aching flesh.

I used to think Casper's breeding kink was just a dirty possessive streak until he confessed he secretly hoped his sperm would be so potent it would miraculously blast through my IUD and knock me up. I stopped letting him come inside me after that argument. To see another man's seed painting over what was once his must be torture, but for me, it's pure pleasure.

Before it drips to the floor, I gather it up and push it inside me. The moans that escape me aren't even for show. It's warm, and obscene, and I love it. I scoop up what I spilled onto my chest and push that inside, too.

With my underwear still in his mouth, Casper moans through the fabric, but I can see his breath quickening the way it usually does when he's about to come. He had no relief from me last night, and unless he got off somewhere else in the house, I know he must be in agony.

His face twists, eyes squeezing shut, hips shaking, and from my spot between his knees I watch in awe as his cock twitches over and over against the strained fabric of his sweatpants. Casper is not average in any sense of the word, and I'm surprised he hasn't burst through them at this point.

His eyes widen, then disappear into the back of his head, his stomach tightening as he unleashes one mighty roar from behind his gag.

Captivated, I watch spurt after spurt flood through the grey material, blooming into a dark, damp patch. It's one of the filthiest things I've ever seen in my life. Knowing I just brought a man to orgasm without even touching him is a rush, though of course I'd never tell him that.

"Oh dear," I laugh, "What a mess you've made."

Standing up, I grip his jaw, and my sticky fingers smear Henry's cum across his cheek. His tongue darts out to taste it and suddenly I want nothing more than to see Casper with Henry's cock in his mouth. I don't even know if that's something he wants. It's never come up before, but neither has handcuffing two men to each other.

This weekend is full of surprises, and I need a minute to myself to process it all.

I bend at the waist to press a kiss to his forehead.

"The keys are somewhere in the box. I'll leave you two to figure this out."

Chapter 16

Henry

SASKIA IS A VISION as she sashays her way up the stairs completely naked, and completely in charge. I've always been in awe of the way she owns a room, steps into her power, but dominating us both like this was something else.

I don't know at what point we ended up holding hands, but Casper's grip threatened to crush mine as he listened to me come in her mouth, and again as he... Well, I don't know. I can't see what's gone on behind me but he sounded like a man being torn apart between agony and ecstasy.

Behind me, he continues to thrash like a caged animal, which I suppose he is. Whatever she did to him has left him a panting, groaning wreck. I squeeze his hands tighter, pulling his focus back to me.

"You OK, Casper?"

He mumbles around whatever she's gagged him with.

"Spit it out," I tell him, trying not to laugh at the double meaning, then blinking hard when I almost pass out at the memory of seeing Saskia take my cum in her mouth. She sucked me so hard I'm still seeing stars.

"She... She... I've never..."

"What happened?"

"She made me come without even touching my dick!" he growls, and I burst out laughing.

"Really?"

"Really," he pants, but before long he's laughing too. "What the fuck? She didn't even take it out. I'm still fully clothed."

I twist to see, but it's useless. His blindfold is on the floor by my foot, so whatever she did to make him react like that must have been exceptional viewing. Saskia's clothes lie in a heap, and my cock twitches at the memory of her slipping her bra off right in front of my face. Feeding her nipple into my mouth. Staring into my eyes as I bit it between my teeth.

And there I am getting hard again.

Our laughter dies when we hear the shower turn on upstairs, and our focus returns to the predicament she's left us in.

"How the fuck do we get out of here?" Casper says, trying to shuffle both of our chairs towards the table.

"Are you cuffed to the chair?" I ask, twisting my wrists and tugging on his.

"I don't think so, only to you."

"OK. Let's try to stand up at the same time. Then we find the keys."

Casper moves to stand, but with his body leaning forward, he hauls mine swiftly backwards, and the bars of the chair dig into my spine.

"Ow! Not like that. We have to go at the same time."

I press my back and shoulders against his for support, both relying on core strength as we attempt to rise like we're part of some fucked up corporate trust exercise. His groan matches mine, but it works. We're on our feet and sidestepping the chairs, but that's only halfway to freedom.

Saskia threw my sweatpants out of reach when she stripped them off me, but she couldn't remove my t-shirt while I was in the cuffs. I look ridiculous, my lower half fully on display, cock jutting out like some filthy version of Winnie the Pooh.

Casper heads for the table, yanking me so hard I bump into his back and almost knock us both over.

"Watch it!" he yells.

"You fucking watch it. I'm walking backwards and I can't see shit, remember? Take it slow."

We shuffle together, positioning ourselves sideways next to where the box sits open and overflowing. Casper takes the lead, lifting my hands with his while he rummages for the keys, flinging toys all over the table. Something bright blue bounces off the edge and onto the floor.

Is that an alien tentacle?

I adjust my angle to get a better look in the box. Fuck, there's some good shit in there. Clamps, floggers, dildos and plugs. I'd feel jealous for all the times the two of them have spent playing together here, were it not for the fact that I know she's mine now, and we still have days to play before I head back.

My stomach drops at the thought of New York, the place I've called home for the past fifteen years. I have a good life there. Great work, great clients, great friends. The one thing missing, the thing that's always been missing, is her.

Saskia is it for me, but we can't pretend we're not living different lives right now. Continuing a relationship between London and New York isn't impossible, but we need this week together to figure out where we go from here. Those kinds of conversations won't be easy with her soon to be ex-husband stomping around the house. Harder still if he's going to be cuffed to me much longer.

"Got them!"

Finally, Casper grabs hold of the keys, shoving them blindly between us, then immediately dropping them onto the floor.

"Oh, fuck you, you dickhead," I groan, throwing my head back and accidentally whacking it into his.

"Who are you calling a dickhead?" he thrashes, headbutting me back. "This is all your fucking fault, you know? If you hadn't turned this into a dick swinging contest, this would never have happened."

"What the fuck are you talking about? You're the one who was acting like you'd need to teach me what to do with a vibrator. You're the one that tipped her over the edge. If this is anyone's fault, it's yours."

He roars behind me, pulling so hard it feels like my shoulder might pop out of the socket. I shove back with all my weight, pushing as hard as I can until he's trapped, writhing between me and the wall. He's strong, but I'm stronger, and a swift elbow to the ribs makes him stop this shit.

"Chill the fuck out, man. We need to get back down to the floor, but we can't do shit with you acting like a bear in a trap the entire time."

I give him a few seconds to let his rage subside before pulling us away from the wall.

"Lean back and we'll squat down together on three, OK?"

"Fine," he says, his weight pressing against me.

"And let me pick them up this time. On three. One... two... three..."

My attempt at a slow descent is thwarted by his sudden squat, and we both end up crashing to the floor in a heap. By a stroke of luck, the keys are just within reach of my fingertips, but he rolls to his side, dragging me with him.

"Hold still! And let me lead."

"Just hurry up!" he yells, as if I'm thrilled at the prospect of rolling around on the floor with my dick out for the rest of the day.

"Shut up. I can't concentrate while you're shouting at me."

Finally, I get a tiny key between my fingers, and carefully push it into one of the locks, but it won't turn. I try the other one, and one cuff springs open on my wrist. Extricating my arms from his, I shove him off me and scramble to my feet, while he, still handcuffed, wrestles himself onto his knees.

I have an opportunity to do the funniest thing here. It's tempting to put the keys out of reach and leave him to it while I follow Saskia to the shower, but he and I share a bond now. In this fucked up escape room, no man is left behind.

"Uncuff me," he pleads, and I crouch behind him to let him go. The second I free one wrist, he bolts, charging for the stairs while the cuffs still hang from the other.

Chapter 17

Henry

"Where are you going?"

"I have to talk to her."

I rush after him, tug him back by the waistband of his trousers, and shove him into the kitchen.

"I think we should give her some space. Just let her shower and get her head together."

His hands fist my t-shirt at the shoulders, his lip curled up into a snarl. "Don't tell me what to do, you bastard."

"Oi!" I snap, pushing him up against the kitchen counter. "You need to cool your head too, mate. Just give her a minute. That was intense for all of us."

In the living room, I find my pants flung across the back of the sofa and tug them up over my hips. Then I wash my hands, run him a glass of water, then one of my own.

"Here, drink that and I'll find us something stronger."

I watch his throat roll as he downs it in one, and my dick, more confused than ever, twitches again. Casper is undeniably attractive, all that Italian machismo bubbling under the surface of skin that sports a year-round tan.

He's quite the picture, standing there with his chest heaving, the front of his sweatpants soaked from Saskia's torment. I can't stop staring at the light grey material turned almost black. I've never seen this man's dick, but I can make out the outline of it where his sweatpants stick to his skin. It's pretty fucking hot on some base level, and I lose track of time staring at it before turning away.

Rummaging through the cupboards, I find a bottle of whisky and pull two glasses from the shelf. I splash three fingers into each, then turn back with a peace offering. Casper stares at me while he takes his first sip, and part of me wonders what it would taste like on his lips.

"Why did you come here?" I ask, and he dismisses me with a shrug. "Come on, mate, we all know that line about spending one last Christmas in the cottage was bullshit. You knew she'd be here, and you knew I was coming too."

His mouth opens and closes as he attempts to speak, but he knows there's no point in lying.

"I think you forgot for a minute there how smart she is. So what was the plan?"

He swirls the whisky around in his glass, throws it back and leans in closer. "There is one thing I could never give her on my own. I thought this would be my last chance to make her happy."

"You mean a threesome?"

"Yeah," he nods, then points back out to the living room. "I just didn't think it would happen like that."

"I don't know what that was, but it wasn't a threesome, by my definition."

His gaze flicks up to mine, eyes narrowing as he gets a read on me.

I've had one before, with two women, not long after Saskia and Casper's wedding. In hindsight, I was avoiding my feelings about it by chasing women all over New York, a debauched couple of years that were nowhere near as satisfying as if I'd approached them with a clear head.

This particular woman and I had been casually dating for a month or two before she suggested her friend join us. I was fully on board, but it pretty quickly became clear they were more interested in each other. I only saw her once after that.

Sleeping with two women was one thing, but two guys has never been a fantasy of mine, not until last night when Casper stood by and watched me react to his ex-wife's touch. Or right now, when I fucked Saskia's mouth with Casper's fingers woven between mine.

"Are you bisexual?" I ask him, and he shrugs dismissively.

"Pleasure is pleasure, my friend. Are you?"

"No," I tell him, keeping the *'I don't think so'* part of that sentence to myself. I'm not ready to suggest otherwise while I'm still processing a lot of feelings about it. My sexuality has never been in question until now.

"You know why we separated?" he asks.

"You wanted different things."

Saskia broke the news of their split over a video call, her tone sombre but measured. Her explanation was brief. He wanted kids, she didn't. She'd clearly accepted their decision, but I'd wanted to crawl through the phone and scoop her into my arms all the same.

"From life, yes," Casper says. "Not from sex. That was never the issue."

"So I gathered from last night. Can I ask you a question?"

"Sure."

"You're both clearly very experienced with all sorts of kinky shit. If this is something she's always wanted, why haven't you done it before? I'm sure you could have found a third person to join you, no problem."

"Use your brain, Henry," he laughs, filling his glass with water, then chugging it down. "You know her. Saskia is fiercely loyal, to a fault at times. She puts everyone else first, her friends, her clients. She put me first, too."

"I don't follow."

"Look, she has loved you her whole life, but as soon as we were married, she buried those feelings deep down."

He continues for a while, but I've stopped listening.

"She loves me?"

"You must see it," he scoffs. "Or you wouldn't be here."

"What do you mean?"

"No man with a face like yours travels across the world just to stick his dick in something. I'm sure you have plenty of women in New York."

"I don't, actually."

"And why is that?"

I don't even pause to answer. "Because there's no one like her."

"You had that wonderful girlfriend a few years ago. What was her name again?"

"Julia," I remind him.

"Why didn't you marry her?"

"Because..."

"Because?" he sing-songs, mocking me. He knows exactly what my answer would be. "Exactly. So don't pretend to me you don't love her, too."

"And you don't?"

"Of course I do. When you have a woman like that, she'll always keep a piece of your heart, even if you decide to let each other go. It's not for lack of love that we have ended our time together, it's because we love each other so much that we're willing to let each other go."

Usually when couples separate, it's because they've drifted apart, or one has wronged the other somehow. Though I believed her when she said it was over, I hadn't known how much I needed to hear him say it, too.

It's good to know he still supports her, but won't be trying to change her mind while she figures out this next phase of her life.

"If you don't get your shit together and tell her you feel the same, don't come complaining to me when some boring finance guy has her on his arm within a year."

The thought turns my stomach. "She wouldn't."

"Do you even want to test that theory?"

No, I fucking don't.

"You're the only man I would do this with, Henry. Once the snow has cleared, I'll be gone, and she'll be so loyal to you, I'm sure she'll never mention it again."

He picks a shiny red apple from the fruit bowl on the counter, washes it, and takes a big bite. My glutes clench at the thought of him sinking his teeth into me instead.

"It will be my one regret that I never fulfilled all of her wishes. Let's give her one more gift. Together. What do you say?"

"If you'd asked me that two days ago I might have punched you in the face, but after what she just did to both of us..." I huff out a long breath, cock twitching—*again*—at the memory of her disappearing out of sight after taking a mouthful of my come. "It feels like she deserves a little special treat in return."

"Revenge?" he says, tapping his fingertips together. "Is that what you're suggesting?"

"You tell me. What would be the best way to get her back, while still making sure she has a great time?"

"Total annihilation," he says, eyebrows pumping up and down.

"Chill out, mate. She's a woman, not a video game."

Our heads turn when we hear the bathroom door open upstairs. Casper tries to leave, but I stop him, one hand splayed across his chest. His skin is warm and smooth, and my fingertips flex instinctively, pressing into his tight muscles.

"Let me go up and check on her. See where her head's at. That snow's not going anywhere, so maybe we just relax tonight and see where tomorrow takes us."

"You're pathetic," he pouts.

"Says the man who just came in his pants."

"That's not fair," he gasps. "You would have done the same if you saw how filthy she looked."

Chapter 18

Saskia

HENRY KNOCKS ON MY bedroom door, and even though he's just seen me naked, I wrap my fluffy towel tightly around my body.

"Come in."

His hair is mussed up from where I gripped handfuls of it while I rode him, but the smile on his face suggests he doesn't care.

"Good shower?"

"Really good, thank you."

Much needed, both physically and mentally. I'm not normally so dominant with one man, let alone two. I was grateful for some space to process what just happened.

He closes the door behind him, and we hear the bathroom door slam shut.

"Is Casper OK?" I ask, panic creeping in that I basically abandoned him. Aftercare is important to me, and that was not it.

"Bit messy," Henry smirks. "He'll survive. Come here, sit with me for a second."

He hops onto the bed and leans back against the headboard, patting the space next to him. I pull my towel tighter and join him, glowing inside at the sight of him in my bed, at last.

It was easy to ignore my feelings for Henry when things were good with Casper. When I was being touched and worshipped so often, there wasn't space in my brain to think about anyone else.

Then, while we were drifting apart, Henry was simply the friend I desperately needed. The shoulder to cry on even if he was thousands of miles across the Atlantic ocean. There was never a text that was left on read, or a 3am call he didn't answer.

Even though we have seventeen years of friendship filled with memories, those nights where we'd video chat in the dim light of our bedrooms are some of the best. When I'd wake at five, he'd be heading to bed, and I could imagine myself there, with my head on his other pillow.

"Last night, you said you haven't been with anyone for a while."

"I haven't. Not since a brief thing last year."

"Were you waiting for me?"

He hums softly and takes a deep breath as he ponders my question. "Not consciously. I wasn't hoping for the downfall of your relationship, if that's what you were thinking?"

"No?"

"No, never. It's more that when I admitted to myself how I felt about you, everyone else might as well have disappeared."

"I think I've been waiting for you," I confess.

"Really?"

A trickle of water drips from my hair down my chest, and he catches it with his fingertip.

"When you told me it was over with Julia, I was strangely happy about it."

"Mean," he teases, rubbing the water into my skin.

"I know. I hated myself for it. And it was extremely confusing for me."

"Don't hate yourself, sweetheart. Julia was fine about the break-up. We were never going to last."

Those envious feelings were buried so deep, there's still a trace of them now. Ugly feelings that twisted my stomach and sat heavy on my heart. I never wanted to feel that way, only wanted what was best for him, even if that wasn't me.

"I would never have admitted as much while you were in a relationship. Or while I was."

"No, neither would I."

"Well, I'm glad we're not in relationships now," I tell him, burrowing my face in the crook of his neck, not caring if my damp hair soaks his t-shirt.

His chest rumbles as he laughs softly and shakes his head.

"What's so funny?"

His grip on my hip tightens, and he pulls me into his lap. "You deluded little thing. We are very much in a relationship now."

"We are?"

"If you think I'm going back to New York as a single man, you're fucking nuts."

His words pierce through the walls I've constructed around my heart, the cage I've trapped my feelings in, in case he didn't feel the same way too. It's too much to even look at him right now, so I hide my face in his neck again.

"I mean it, Saskia. It's you and me now. I know this week isn't exactly giving us the time we both need to talk and figure things out, but I'm beginning to wonder how much of that we need, anyway. It's clear as day I'm absolutely crazy about you."

His fingers tip my chin up so he can look me in the eye and make sure I understand him. My lips are a little sore from kissing so intensely downstairs, but I let him take them gently. Soft and slow, in a way we haven't been with each other so far.

"I have a gift for you," he whispers against my mouth.

"Henry, you didn't have to."

"Do you really think I was going to come all the way from New York empty-handed?"

He climbs off the bed and returns with a box I recognise from a luxury lingerie boutique in Manhattan.

"I had planned to give it to you on Christmas morning, but I rather like the idea of you having it early."

"And why is that?"

"Open it and you'll see."

There, nestled amongst delicate sheets of tissue paper, is the most exquisite lace lingerie set. A forest green thong with double straps on the sides, and a matching bra so sheer my nipples tighten, already knowing how easy it will be to see them when it's on.

"This is gorgeous. Should I put it on now?"

"Tomorrow," he says, slipping the lid back on the box. "I think we should give your body a rest for tonight, and I've told Casper the same."

"Oh, so you've been talking about me, have you?" Henry pulls me closer and kisses my bare shoulder.

"Maybe a little bit."

"Let me guess. He wants revenge?"

"How did you know?"

My pulse races at the thought of the two of them plotting. There won't be enough hours left in the day to get into all the ways I've been reprimanded for misbehaving in the past.

"Because I don't do things like that and get away with it."

"And you're OK with that?" he asks, dipping his head to look me straight in the eyes. "A little payback?"

"Very little is off limits with Casper and I. Or *was*," I correct myself. "It would be the same with you."

"I'd hoped I'd be able to figure your limits out myself," he says, kissing his way along the slope of my neck.

On the one hand, Casper's antics have robbed us of a chance to take our time, but on the other, we've been thrown in at the deep end, and when it feels this good, it can't be a bad thing.

"When he told you he'd be the best person to teach you what I like, he had a good point. You already know I love surprises. Whatever the two of you have in mind, I'm sure I can handle it."

Chapter 19
Casper

WHEN WE WERE STILL together, our Christmas Day tradition was a long walk through the countryside before coming home to light a fire and hide from the world.

Saskia would curl up with a book or sit at the table with her jigsaw puzzle. I'd open a bottle of wine and make a start on preparing dinner with orchestral carols on the radio.

There might be music and wine, but this year couldn't be more different.

Henry and I are on the sofa with our feet up, but while he looks relaxed and comfortable, I'm coiled like a fucking spring. I've been watching the two of them make puppy-dog eyes at each other all morning, and she's been flouncing around in her robe knowing fine well I can't slip my hands inside like I used to.

Normally she'd cover up in cashmere loungewear, so I feel like she's up to something. I just can't figure it out while she keeps her distance.

At the dining table, she strings together even more paper chains. As if she hasn't already decorated enough.

She likes to do things like this when she's here, to keep her hands busy and her mind off of work. Surely work is the last thing on her mind while the three of us are in a room together. I can think of plenty of other ways to keep her hands busy.

My thoughts are solely focused on the three of us getting naked, but Henry and I haven't had a moment together today to come up with our payback plan. I can't exactly ask him to step outside with me while the snow is still coming down.

I shift, leaning over the back of the sofa, impatient for her attention.

"Hey, what are you wearing underneath your robe?"

"Wouldn't you like to know?" she says, taking a sip of her wine and refusing to look my way.

"Yes, I would. That's why I asked."

"I know what she's wearing," Henry says from the other end of the sofa, still working on his crossword.

"What the fuck? How does he get to know, and I don't?"

"Because I bought it for her, and I was there when she put it on."

She bites back her smile, certain she has the upper hand. She doesn't, unless Henry has swapped allegiances again, which he'd better fucking not have. For these games with Saskia, I need him on my side.

"I want to see it," I tell him. "What do you think, Henry? Can I take a look?"

"Be my guest," he shrugs.

"Henry!" Saskia shrieks as I leap up and make my way over to where she sits. She picks up another strip of paper, refusing to look my way.

"What?" he laughs. "I think I'd rather enjoy letting him look at what he can't have anymore. Wasn't that your plan for him yesterday? To show him once and for all that you're not his."

Saskia's eyes flare and her bottom lip disappears behind her teeth. Henry folds his newspaper away and leaves the comfort of the sofa to join us by the table. I move behind her, lifting her hair to pull it back into a ponytail, wrapping it gently around my fist.

"That really was very naughty of you," Henry says, tracing his fingers down her cheek to her neck, then slipping the robe off one shoulder. "I suspect your husband is keen for a little payback for that filthy game you made him play with us."

"Ex-husband," she huffs out, nuzzling her cheek against his palm.

I yank her hair hard, forcing her to look up at me, and the robe slips further. His hand drifts to her throat and she smiles, eyes turning hazy.

"What do you think, Casper? Have we got time to play with our toy?"

"We're snowed in on Christmas Day, my friend. We've got nothing but time."

Saskia's chest heaves, and Henry tugs at the belt-tie, pulling it free and letting it fall further.

I wish I knew him well enough to read his mind right now.

"Get her on the table," he says to me, gripping her elbow and hauling her out of her chair.

Fuck yes.

Saskia took charge yesterday. I led the way the night before, but now is Henry's moment to shine. And I, for one, can't wait to see what he's made of.

"No, no, no!" she squeals in protest, but still hopping up to sit on the edge. "You'll squash my paper chains."

Henry surprises me by sweeping them to the floor, but then he pauses, picks them up, and waves a string of them in her face.

"How do these work?"

"You loop the strips through each other and close them with a sticky strip."

"Think we could restrain her with these?" he asks me, a wide grin spread across his face.

Saskia bursts out laughing. "Wow, is that the best you two can come up with?"

"Lie down and put your arms above your head."

"You're not serious."

"Deadly serious, sweetheart. On your back. Now."

Saskia pulls her robe tight around her again, but it's useless, and it falls open as soon as she lies back. I watch as Henry fastens a chain around one wrist, then the other, before picking up the strands she's already made and connecting those too.

"Are you cold?" Henry asks, his face close to hers.

"A little."

"Your nipples look like they could cut glass." He flicks one with the tip of his finger and she gasps at the sensation while he turns his attention back to me. "Chain her ankles."

From the foot of the table, I nudge her legs apart and find the narrow strip between her legs damp, fabric plastered to her pussy.

"You're soaked, angel. What's that all about?"

"Can you blame me?" she laughs, wiggling to find a comfortable position while I wrap another paper chain strip around her slender ankle.

I may be an artist, but my medium is paint and my work is expansive, I don't fuck around with fiddly little things like paper chains.

It takes a little while to fasten them all in place, but soon her wrists and ankles are chained to decorations that trail off the edges and are secured tightly to each table leg.

"This underwear was an excellent choice," I tell Henry, who joins me at the foot of the table and slaps me on the back.

"Thanks, mate. Appreciate that."

He acts like I've complimented him on his own attire, dark jeans and a tight fitting top he's pushed up at the sleeves.

We take a moment to admire our handiwork. Bound to the table, our plaything is exactly where we want her. Saskia is a heavenly vision, her long, silky hair spilling over her shoulders. There's a reason I've always called her my angel.

"What do we do now?" I ask him.

"Now we watch Die Hard."

"What?" I scoff.

Is this man crazy?

We have the most beautiful woman on earth tied up for our pleasure, and he wants to watching a fucking action film?

"Why?"

"Because it's a great Christmas movie," he shrugs.

"It is not a Christmas movie," Saskia laughs. "And don't be ridiculous. You need to teach me my lesson. Isn't that your plan?"

He tuts loudly and delivers a sudden spank between her legs that has both her and me gasping.

"I don't think you get what you want today."

He walks over to the sofa, picks up the remote, and props his feet up on the coffee table.

"You can't leave me here like this!" Saskia yells, her eyes pleading with me.

I'm frozen to the spot, unsure of what to do. Normally, I would never leave her tied up somewhere. It's not safe, or responsible, but these are paper chains, for fuck's sake. We all know she's not really restrained right now.

"You can get up whenever you like, angel," I reassure her.

"She could," Henry says. "But she won't. Sit down, Casper."

Why does everyone in this house keep telling me to sit down?

"What happens if I get up?" she asks, lifting her head to look at him. I follow her gaze across the room, and Henry twists to stare at me, his eyebrows lifting just a fraction. Our agreement may be unspoken, but

I know we're on the same page here. Saskia must pay, and the price is her pleasure.

"If you break those chains, I'll bend you over and spank you until you're wearing nothing but my handprint," I tell her.

Her laughter fills the air, but I see goosebumps prickling on her arms. I've had her bent over this very table several times and she's always thoroughly enjoyed herself.

"Oh, how awful," she says sarcastically. "I would absolutely hate that."

"That's not what I have in mind," Henry says, remote in hand, his voice filled with menace.

"What are you thinking?" I ask.

"Hang on, I'm just finding somewhere to watch the movie."

Saskia and I wait with bated breath, her chest rising and falling, while he finds what he's looking for.

"A-ha!" he says, loading it up, then pressing pause.

He sets the remote down and returns to my side to trace one fingertip slowly from the inside of her thigh, up over the curve of her belly. Saskia writhes and twitches underneath his touch, her body responding everywhere he goes. Up and up, he continues, kicking chairs aside as he stalks his way around the table.

He strokes between her beautiful breasts, sliding up the long slope of her neck and past her chin. When he reaches her lips, she darts her tongue out to catch a taste of his flesh, and he squeezes her face, forcing her to look up at him.

"If you break those chains, I won't touch you. And I won't let Casper touch you, either." I watch the toned muscles of her thighs twitch at his words. "You'll spend the rest of this trip naked and aching, and we'll never let you come."

Watching him tease her like this is hypnotic, and I think perhaps Henry didn't need my lessons after all.

"You wouldn't," she whimpers.

"Try me," he says.

Chapter 20

Saskia

IT WOULD TAKE NO effort to shred the paper chains they've carefully fastened around my limbs. It will, however, take great effort to make sure they stay intact so I don't break their silly little rule. There's enough give to move a little, but I'd have more range of movement if they took me to bed with the cuffs we have in our toy box.

Being restrained is something I've always enjoyed, and Casper and I have played plenty, but never like this, and never with the threat of being left alone. It's a thrill for a few minutes, but not for however long Die Hard lasts. I've seen it once, years ago, and can't for the life of me remember whether it's a quick movie or one that drags on for hours.

"You can't leave me here like this," I protest. Surely they aren't going to watch television while I'm laid out like a feast?

"You didn't tell me she had such a bratty side," Henry says to Casper.

"Oh yes, she can be quite a rude little cunt when she wants to be."

They stand on either side of the table, arms folded, staring down at me. Hearing them speak about me as if I'm not even here should infuriate me. In a work setting, I'd be apoplectic, but here it only makes me feel feral.

"What if I need to pee?" I ask.

I don't, but if I'm expected to lie here for hours, I probably will.

"Then pee," Henry shrugs, and Casper and I both gasp.

"Oh, she's definitely not into that," he tells Henry.

"Fine, then she can hold it in until we've had our fun with her."

"You bastard," I sneer up at him.

Henry squats beside me, his expression frustratingly neutral. I might be protesting, but I love the thrill of not knowing how he's going to respond.

"I'm not a fan of this attitude, Saskia," he says calmly. "I'd rather see you use your manners."

He strokes his fingers through my hair. Back and forth, back and forth, an exquisite scalp massage that only serves to turn me on even more.

"I won't hurt you, and I won't let him hurt you, either. I promise. Do you have a safe word?"

"With Casper, yes."

"Do you want a new one with me?" I nod, trying to stay focused on Henry while Casper trails his fingertips up and down the inside of my leg. "What's your word with him?"

"Rudolph," Casper answers for me. "Our special one for Christmas in the cottage."

He dips his head to kiss just above my belly-button, and I wonder what he thinks of all this. Of Henry running the show when normally he's the one in control.

"That's cute," Henry smiles. "Then we'll have another reindeer to keep things simple. But which one should it be? Dasher, Dancer, Prancer..."

"Jupiter!" Casper chimes in, and Henry's fingers pause at my hair-line.

"Jupiter is a planet, Casper. Not a reindeer."

"Oh. Is it Jingles then?"

Henry stands and rests his palms flat on the table. "Are you winding me up? Jingles the reindeer? It's Dasher and Dancer and Prancer and... and... shit."

"Blizzard," Casper says, clicking his fingers.

"Not Blizzard, but Blitzen, thank you! Then Comet and Cupid and Donner and... fuck, what's the last one?"

Henry folds his arms across his chest and taps his foot. His expression is like the one I see when he's engrossed in a crossword, not the one I want to see when I'm waiting to have sex.

The pair of them stand over me, mulling it over, repeating the names until they all sound made up.

Casper paces by my side. "I'm sure it begins with a V. Velvet? Venus? Veronica?"

"Vixen!" I shout. "For fuck's sake. It's Vixen."

"Yes, that's it!" Henry says, and they high-five across the table like they got there themselves. "Vixen it is. You want out of here, you just say the word. We'll wrap you in blankets and snuggle you between us on the sofa."

"That sounds nice," I moan, my arms already feeling a little tingly.

"It does sound nice, doesn't it? And we can do that later anyway, but first we want to have a little fun with you. I want you all needy and desperate."

"But I *am* needy and desperate."

Henry adjusts the obvious bulge in the front of his jeans and clears his throat.

"What will it be, Saskia? Are you going to be a good girl for us and stay still, or are you going to keep acting like a horny little bitch?"

I knew from the way he went down on me the other night that he's good with his mouth, but I didn't know he'd be so good at dirty talk. I want more, and perhaps playing along is the best way to get it.

"Fine," I sigh. "I'll be a good girl."

"That's what I thought." He strokes his fingertips down the length of my arm, eyes locked on mine as he flicks my nipple again. "I think we'll blindfold you, too."

Fuck, fuck, fuck.

Everything tightens at the thought and I'd be tempted to tear right out of the chains if I didn't know that Henry is a man of his word.

If he says he's going to do something, he always follows through. The thought of him not touching me for the rest of the week is unbearable. I need him touching me now, constantly, every day until I die.

The box of toys Casper brought down yesterday is still nearby, and I angle my head to watch Henry rifle through it.

Holy shit.

They're going to touch me while I'm blindfolded, and I won't know who is who. This is the dirtiest, darkest fantasy I have. It's buried so deep in my core, I've never told a soul, not even Casper.

But Henry knows. He just knows.

Once he finds what he's looking for, he slips it over my face, adjusting the tension and plunging me into darkness. A few seconds later, I feel a soft kiss pressed against the inside of my thigh, teeth sinking into my flesh, then Henry's wet tongue, soothing away the pain.

At least, I think it's his tongue.

Chapter 21

Saskia

Time loses all meaning when you're bound and blindfolded. Now and then I hear them whispering, conspiring. I hold my breath, willing my heartbeat to quieten so I can make out their words. Their plans for me.

Trying to follow along with the movie is pointless, and Casper and Henry take great delight in their silent teasing.

On the way to the kitchen, someone tickles the exposed inside of my thighs, then later someone else—*or the same person, who knows?*—drags their nails down them, hard enough I'm sure they've left a mark.

One of them pulls the cups of my bra down, but then I feel a mouth on each nipple, sucking so hard I almost rip the chains. If they kept it up, I could probably come from that alone. I whine when they release me too soon, working together to attach a clamp to one nipple, then the other.

"I hate you," I moan, and they suppress their laughs as they leave me again.

At one point, Henry makes microwave popcorn, and I can tell it's him from the way he hums to himself in the kitchen. The warm, buttery smell fills the cottage and my stomach rumbles even though I ate a decent breakfast. Just when I think he's about to head back to the sofa, I sense him pause at the foot of the table.

"Open your mouth," he orders, and I open wide, just in time for a piece of popcorn to bounce off my forehead. "Oh dear, better luck next time, sweetheart."

I'm about to snap back with some bitchy retort when suddenly his voice is close to my ear, his breath tickling my cheek.

"I'd have eaten your cunt if you'd caught that."

He licks my mouth, dragging his warm tongue across the seam of my lips, pulling away before I can kiss him back. I suck at my lips, one at a time, desperate for the salty taste of him. Anything to tide me over while I ride out their torture.

Later, just as the action picks up on the television, I hear one of them fetch beers from the kitchen, dropping two bottle caps into the sink.

Casper.

I've told him a thousand times to stop doing that.

He pauses between my spread thighs, and I listen carefully to the sound of bubbles fizzing in the bottle, his throat rolling as he swallows a long pull.

Knowing he's watching me is a huge turn on, and I wonder what I must look like from his perspective. Is my skin flushed? Can he see how much I'm throbbing between my legs?

I expect him to leave me again, but when he presses the cold bottle against the inside of my thigh, I yelp and almost break the chains. He drags it up and pushes it hard against my damp underwear. I've never wanted to fuck something so much in my life.

"Do you need to use your safe word, angel?"

Part of me wants out of here. I know I could use it and they'd stop all of this teasing and tormenting. The other part of me knows the pay-off will be phenomenal, so I shake my head, and he goes.

Despite being almost naked, the fire keeps the room warm, and I think about letting myself nap, but I'm too excited to switch off. My limbs, trembling with anticipation, begin to ache, and I know I'll feel stiff tomorrow.

Finally, I hear *Let it Snow* and the end credits roll.

"Such a great film," Henry says. "Shall we make it a double bill?"

"Don't you fucking dare," I cry out.

If they start another movie, I'll break out of these chains and make myself come before they can do anything about it. I don't care about the consequences. I don't even need them at this point. One touch of my clit would be all it takes to make myself go off like a rocket.

"Did you hear something?" Casper laughs, and I could kill Henry for laughing along with him.

"No, I don't think I did."

Two sets of footsteps stalk towards me, sending a fresh batch of goosebumps zipping all over my skin. Casper wasn't lying when he told Henry how much I love the anticipation of being touched, of being pleasured, but this has gone too far now.

"I think it was a needy little slut," Casper says. "Have you seen one around here?"

Warm hands palm my legs, stroking up and down, but nowhere close to where I want them.

"What do you think, Casper?" Henry says, and my ears place his voice further away. "Should we give her our gift and fuck both her holes tonight?"

I clench around nothing, shocked at how much it turns me on to hear them plotting against me as if I'm not right here laid out before them. Henry hums, and that simple noise alone feels like an exquisite threat.

"I think she might need a little preparation," Casper answers.

"Do you have anything we could use to get her ready for us?"

They rummage in the toy box, and I know full well there is a selection of plugs he could choose from. I like the pink glass bulb best, but Casper is all about the visuals, and I know he likes a larger plug with a flared base and a heart jewel.

We picked it up on a trip to Paris years ago, and he made me wear it to dinner. That was the night I confessed how much I longed to have all my holes filled at once, to give my body over to the most depraved cravings.

When he vowed to make it happen, I hadn't believed him, assuming it was a promise uttered in a moment of ecstasy, soon to be forgotten. Clearly, it's never left his mind.

"Do you need to use the bathroom before we begin?" he asks, stroking the backs of his fingertips down my stomach. Casper is a well-seasoned pro when it comes to anal play, and if there's one piece of knowledge I'd want him to pass on to Henry, it's that it takes a little time to work me up to it.

"I'm all good," I answer, a little distracted by the thought of taking them both later. "I'm ready."

The squelch of a bottle of lube drags me back into the present, and I yelp at the sensation of cold, slick metal pressing against me. The pressure, then the stretch, does little to quell the ache that's been building for god knows how long.

I learned early on that taking away one of my senses skyrockets everything else. If I can't use my hands, my body is thrumming with the need to be touched. If I can't see, my ears are on alert for even the tiniest of aural clues. My imagination runs wild, and I have an almost out-of-body experience picturing us from all angles of the room.

There's no way to tell what they're doing right now, but the vision of them both squatting to watch the plug open me up almost makes me come on the spot.

"Now then," Henry muses. "I can't decide whether to deny her orgasms or give her so many it makes her cry."

A ragged sob escapes me. "You've been denying me for the full length of a movie. If you keep this up, I'll cry anyway."

"What'll it be, Casper?" Henry asks.

"Well," he sighs. "As much as I like the idea of making her wait, our time here is limited. It would be a shame for us to not make the most of it."

"Hmm, great point." His fingers tug the elastic on my underwear, snapping it against my skin. "We should have taken these off because we put your chains on. I'll have to cut them off."

"No, you just gave them to me!" I protest.

"I'll buy you another pair."

His footsteps retreat, and I hear the kitchen drawer open and close before the *snip-snip* of the sides being cut. He yanks them out from underneath me, tossing them aside. He drops to the floor, and I feel the warmth of his breath ghosting over my aching flesh, his tongue sweeping through me, and behind my blindfold, I see stars.

Chapter 22

Henry

THIS IS THE BEST Christmas ever.

My beautiful woman is squirming on my tongue, gasping for breath, and utterly helpless to do anything about it. While I fuck her with my tongue, my palms keep her hips pinned, and Casper watches me from the head of the table, practically drooling.

He leans over her, removing the clamps from her nipples and sucking each into his mouth while she muffles her moans against his chest.

"Can I come?" she begs.

"Any time you like," I tell her, and she goes off like a rocket before I even wrap my lips around her clit and suck hard. Pressed to the table, all she can do is jerk against my mouth as she falls apart, hips twisting and convulsing as I keep it up.

I pull away, panting for breath, and slide two fingers inside her.

"Can she squirt?" I ask Casper, and his eyes light up.

"Oh yes, she can. Question is, can she do it without breaking her chains?"

"Why don't we find out?"

Curling them upwards, I rock my hand in and out of her in a coaxing motion.

"More," she whines.

"More fingers? I might need a helping hand, Casper."

He rounds the table, joining me to push two of his own inside her. My jaw drops at the sight of us both stretching her open. It's insanely hot, but she's so wet our soaked fingers can't find the right rhythm and we keep pushing each other out.

Casper grabs my wrist, brings my fingers to his mouth and sucks them clean. My cock throbs at the sight of him swallowing the taste of her. Of us.

"We have a glass dildo that always gets her there," he says.

"Get it. Now."

He lifts the box onto the table and quickly finds what he's looking for, cleaning it off with a hygiene wipe. It's long and clear, with a bulbous tip that looks so pretty as I work it inside her.

"That feel good, Sass? You doing OK?"

"So good. Don't stop."

"Casper, I think you might need to hold her down for this."

He presses one hand just beneath her belly-button, the other gripping her thigh in his large palm. I angle the toy upwards and pick up the pace.

"Oh fuck," she moans. "Oh fuck, oh fuck, oh fuck."

She does her best to breathe deeply and stay in control, but her moan soon shifts to a roar, then a whine, then a strangled cry as the pressure becomes too much to bear.

I pull the toy out just as she explodes, the spray of liquid soaking the front of my shirt.

Casper looks on in awe, then pushes me aside, dropping between her thighs to lap up what's left on her skin. I move to the top of the table and bend to kiss her, letting her control the pace as she rides one orgasm out and straight into another. Her breath is ragged against my mouth, so I just press my cheek to hers while she comes down from her high.

"Shhh, baby, shhh," I say, stroking her hair and adjusting her blindfold where it slipped a little. "You did so good."

Casper strips out of his clothes, then comes up behind me, tugging the hem of my top up and over my head. His hand moves to unzip my jeans, but I stop him before he can push them off my hips.

"I want to keep her coming while we take turns using her mouth. Do you have anything that will do the job?"

Saskia whimpers, and he searches for more fun treats.

"I don't know if it's charged," he says, just as the small egg-shaped vibrator buzzes to life in his hand. He cleans it off and pushes it inside her, making her back arch off the table. Her elbows shoot down to her sides, tearing the chains apart.

"I'm sorry, I'm sorry!" she yells, clearly panicking about our earlier threat. Honestly, I'm impressed she kept still all this time, but she'll be well rewarded for it later.

"It's OK. I think you're ready for a new position, anyway. Casper, grab a cushion."

Saskia hugs her arms around her body, visibly relieved at having her full range of movement back. I carefully tear the paper strips off her wrists, do the same for her ankles, then help her off the table and onto her knees.

"Blindfold stays on, OK?"

"OK. I... I..." she struggles, swallowing hard.

"Do you need to use your safe word, angel?" Casper asks.

"No! Definitely not. Just... some water, please?"

I fetch a glass from the kitchen and carefully tip some into her mouth, catching the spilled drops with my thumb. When she's done, I down the rest.

"Thank you," she pants, reaching behind her back to remove her bra. Though her tits have been exposed for a while now, it's incredible to see her like this, kneeling and obedient, in nothing but a blindfold. She scoops her hair behind her shoulders, straightens her back and folds her hands in her lap.

"You know what I think this Christmas needs, Henry?" Casper says, his tone low and teasing. She can't see it, but his grin is both wolfish and playful. He's having a lot of fun, and so am I.

"What's that now?" I ask, matching his energy.

"A little game of Guess Who?"

"Ah, a classic. You want to play Sass?" I ask, sweeping my thumb across her cheek as she nods. "Then be a good girl, open your mouth, and see if you can guess whose cock you're gagging on."

Chapter 23

Henry

CASPER GOES FIRST, AND I have the pleasure of watching her spit on his cock, then making it disappear. It's a mental image I'll never forget, and I almost fall over while slipping out of my jeans because I can't look away.

"Guess who?" he says, his head tipped back, a look of sheer bliss on his face.

It will be easy to place the owner based on the voice coming directly from above her, so I shift closer behind him, rest my chin on his shoulder and join in.

"Guess who?" we both say at the same time.

"Take the blindfold off," she begs before he pushes deeper, making her gag a little.

"Guess who?" I say again. She tries to answer, but it's impossible when her lips are stretched around him, and he's nudging his way down the back of her throat.

"Sorry, I can't hear you," he laughs. "You shouldn't talk with your mouth full. Terrible manners." He slaps her cheek lightly, rubbing at where his swollen head pushes against it from the other side.

"Yours," she attempts to mumble around his girth and he releases her with a wet pop.

"Try again."

"Yours, Casper," she gasps. "Yours."

"That's right. You'll never forget it either." He reaches behind her head and rips the blindfold free. She blinks rapidly as he comes back into view, standing over her, all golden skin and soft hair.

Her eyes flit back and forth between our faces, then down to where one of my hands is splayed across Casper's stomach, the other wrapped around his shaft, as I feed it into her mouth. Pre-cum beads at the tip of my own cock, hard against his ass, and I'm not sure I've ever been this turned on in my life.

Casper pulls out of her mouth and steps aside to make room for me to get closer. He cups her chin gently, adjusting the angle of her head.

"Taste him," he tells her.

She wraps her warm lips around me and I grip the edge of the table to keep my knees from buckling. Her eager tongue swirls, coating me with the spit Casper worked up in her mouth. His hand fists her hair, but it's more for show than for force, and he guides her up and down my length. She's the hottest thing I've ever seen, staring up at me with wide, hungry eyes.

The second hottest thing I've ever seen is Casper standing by my side, stroking himself in smooth motions as he watches his ex-wife work another man's cock into her throat.

"Want both," Saskia moans around me, reaching for Casper's hip to pull him closer. We shuffle together until she squeezes our shafts in one hand. Her tongue laps back and forth between us until she stretches her lips around them both.

Casper groans deeply, looping his arm around my waist to pull me to his side. My hips buck, sliding in and out of Saskia's hot, wet mouth in tandem with his, and I almost blow my load when he traces the shell of my ear with his tongue.

"Don't look at her," he whispers. "Look at me while you come down her throat."

I twist until our foreheads press together and his eyes bore into mine, spurring me on. In my peripheral vision I see Saskia's knees shift apart, her other hand diving between them and working herself in fast circles.

We wanted to overstimulate her, and with the plug, the vibrator, her fingers on her clit and our cocks in her mouth, that's exactly what happens. She comes again, her body writhing, and her deep moan humming through me as she sucks even harder.

"Cass," I moan, not even caring that I've said the wrong name.

He pulls out of her mouth, grabs the back of my neck, and crashes his lips to mine.

I grip him in the same spot, opening for his tongue and feverishly kissing him back. It's different, firmer, a more masculine taste that has the base of my spine tingling as my orgasm edges closer.

This feels inevitable, as if his true purpose in coming here was for me to experience this, not her.

When he bites my bottom lip, it catapults me over the edge and while Saskia drains every drop from me, Casper swallows my moans. Wet heat floods my cock and I look down to see him coming in hot bursts over the two of us. Some lands on her face, some coats my shaft, and Saskia, my queen, laps it all up.

I barely have a second to process all the ways my world just shifted before she removes the vibrator, scrambles to her feet, and leads both of us towards the stairs.

Chapter 24

Saskia

I'VE LOST COUNT OF the number of orgasms I've had, but I know I want more.

Need more.

Never want to stop having orgasms, actually.

I'm practically incoherent, my blood coursing through my veins, chest heaving with every breath. They've well and truly scrambled my brain, and all I can do is squirm in the middle of the bed while they stand at the foot of it, watching over me.

What the hell are they waiting for?

"Should we take a break?" Henry asks, and a thin whine catches in the back of my throat. "We need your words, darling."

"No, no, no." I get up on my knees and shuffle towards them, cupping their cheeks in my palms. Rough stubble has grown in while we've been ignoring the world, and they look hotter than ever. "I want you now. Both of you."

Casper laughs. "Henry, she can handle it. I promise."

"Are you sure?"

"So sure." I run my hands down their chests to their stomachs, and when they both groan deeply, I wonder if it's them who should be taking a break, not me.

"Do I have your permission to fuck her?" Casper asks Henry, looping an arm around his shoulder.

"It's not my permission you need. It's hers."

"Can I, angel?"

This would be the perfect moment to get my revenge, to tell them no, they can't touch me now. They wouldn't be happy about it, but I know they'd respect my wishes. But no, I couldn't do that, because right now there is nothing I want more than both of them inside me.

Holy crap, this is actually happening.

All my dirtiest wishes are about to come true, and I don't know where to begin. The possibilities are... well, not endless, but certainly extensive.

It never occurred to me, because I never actually thought this would happen, to think about who should go in what order, or where. Casper certainly has the most experience with anal, at least with me, but I don't want Henry to think I don't want that from him.

"You can," I tell Casper. "But we left the lube downstairs. Can you grab it, please?"

He heads for the door, and I pull Henry closer, knowing I don't have long.

"Henry, would it be OK if..." I trail off.

Oh gosh, this is awkward to ask.

"What is it, darling?"

"It's just, this is goodbye for me and Casper, so I want to experience as much as possible with him before he leaves."

Henry bites down on his bottom lip, and I can practically feel the heat pouring off of him. I love how much this is turning him on. He grips my shoulders while I reach down and begin stroking his semi-hard length.

"You and I have all the time in the world to explore together. Tonight is all about you, so you can fuck whoever you want, however you want."

"Thank you," I beam up at him, grateful he understands.

He moves to sit at the head of the bed, guiding me up towards him, then angles his knees out to the side and pats his thigh.

"Rest your head here," he says. "I want you to watch me get hard again while he fucks you from behind."

Obediently, I get into position, keeping my knees together and my shoulders low. Henry scoops my hair away from my face and strokes it gently. This could just as easily be the two of us getting ready for an evening of fun together, but the door opens behind me and a shiver zips down my spine.

"Holy fuck," Casper groans when he sees me bent over, ass high in the air and waiting for him.

"Casper," Henry says. "You're up, mate."

Casper tosses the bottle of lube onto the bed and crouches behind me to fill my aching pussy with his tongue. My back arches but Henry palms the side of my head, keeping me pinned to his thigh.

With his other hand, as promised, he caresses himself, stroking his balls, then his shaft, working himself back to full stiffness.

It's a beautiful thing to witness up close, and I take mental notes on the kind of touch and pressure he likes.

Casper gives me his fingers next, spreading my wetness all around and stroking my clit with the deft precision he's honed over the years. He knows exactly how to tease me and keep me on the edge, but this isn't that. This is the touch of a man who wants me to fall apart, and fast.

"Don't fight it," he says. "Come on these fingers, then I'll fuck you right through it."

My mouth opens against Henry's thigh, and he angles his cock to smear pre-cum over my lips.

"You're doing so good, baby," he says, his grip tightening in my hair. "Come for your husband, then we'll give you everything you want."

He knows it's over with Casper, but hearing him say the word *'husband'* adds an extra filthy layer to all of this. The idea of another man joining us in bed, telling us both what to do to each other, is something I've always found unspeakably hot.

And just like that, Henry reads my mind.

"Spank her cunt," he tells Casper, and it only takes one sharp smack for me to fall apart, my thighs trembling as my orgasm floods through every part of me. He doesn't stop there, and I take three, four, five while gasping for air.

Henry wraps his hand around my neck, just enough to keep me from moving. "Shhh, good girl. You can take it."

"I don't know why you're shushing her," Casper laughs, bringing his hand down to spank one ass-cheek and then the other. "I love to hear her get loud."

He adjusts his position and thrusts deep inside me, his own pleasure roaring out of him as he begins to fuck me hard.

Henry strokes himself right in front of me, and while I watch his face, his is solely focused on watching Casper.

His expression shifts subtly, from lust to confusion, then back again, and I feel blessed to witness whatever he's going through right now. He bites his lip and squeezes himself hard.

"God, I'm so fucking close already," Casper moans. "Are you ready to take my cock in your ass, angel?"

He grips both cheeks firmly and spreads me apart, tapping the plug I've been wearing this entire time.

I wiggle my hips back towards him as Henry slaps the head of his cock against my tongue. I wish he'd give me more of it, but he keeps my head still, and I can tell he's enjoying teasing me with it.

"Henry, lie down," Casper says, and from behind me I hear him squirting lube into his palm and coating himself with it.

Henry shifts down the bed, his legs between mine, nudging them apart until I'm hovering above him, ready to sit down for the ride of my life. He rubs his swollen head against my clit, and I throw my head back, certain I could come again just from that light pressure.

Instead, I cover his hand with mine and guide him inside me, gasping at the fullness I feel just from him and the toy. His breath shudders and he pulls me down to kiss him. We stay like that for a minute, Casper's hands roaming my backside as he watches us.

"Fuck, that's a good view," he says. "I love this plug in you. Remember Paris?"

"I remember," I moan, and Henry bites my lip.

Casper eases it out gently, sets it on the nightstand, then lines himself up behind me. Henry reaches down to help spread me apart, and I rest my head against his shoulder and close my eyes.

"Relax baby. Just breathe," Casper says, nudging the head of his lubed up cock inside.

"Look at me. I want to see your face when we both fill you," Henry pleads, and I lift a little. Our mouths are so close, our moans mingle as we feel the pressure of Casper easing all the way in.

One man inside me is heaven, two is blowing my mind. I feel so incredibly full, so overwhelmed by the sensation.

Henry squeezes his eyes shut, and when I look back over my shoulder, Casper does the same, breathing deeply as he adjusts to the pressure. We've done this before with toys, but that was nothing like this. This is another level, so intense I can't think straight.

"Oh my god," I groan. "It's too good. I don't—"

"Do you want us to stop?" Henry asks.

"No, but I don't think I can move."

Casper's warm hand strokes up and down my spine. "It's OK, angel, we've got you. Sit up a little and we'll take care of you."

I plant my hands on either side of Henry's head, and they both grip my hips at the same time. Glancing down, I see them entwined there, working together to lift me up and down. Their hips begin to thrust slowly in tandem until we find a rhythm that works.

Henry looks up at me, fighting to focus as he loses himself to his own pleasure. "Look at you. My beautiful girl. His girl. Taking us both so well."

They pick up their pace, working together to get all of us there at the same time. I close my eyes and give into every sensation. The stretch of my body. The sounds of their moans. The taste of sweat on Henry's skin.

When another orgasm begins to build inside me, I don't reach down and force myself to get there fast, I let myself come like a river. A smooth flow rather than a crashing wave, my body floating along, guided by something outside of my control.

"Where do you want us?" Henry asks.

"Fill me with come," I whimper, the tingling gold rush flooding my limbs as I drop into another plane of existence and let them use my body for their own gains.

Their hands grip and grab at me, and at each other. I lay my head on Henry's shoulder as they fuck me hard, their gasping moans filling my ears. The sensation of them pouring into me simultaneously is like nothing I ever could have imagined.

Henry hugs me tight to his chest and Casper topples forward, sandwiching me between them and capturing Henry's mouth with his. I come down to the sound of their kisses, and I know this is one Christmas I'll never forget.

Chapter 25

Casper

AFTERWARDS, SASKIA LAYS BETWEEN us and we take turns kissing her as we all recover from the high of the last few hours.

Still, Henry and I can't stop touching her, and our hands stroke wherever they can, squeezing her breasts and thighs, and each other too.

We both moan when we find our hands between her legs, playing with the mess we've made, our cum-drenched fingers slipping inside her once more.

My body is thoroughly wrung out, yet I feel like I'm floating on a cloud.

"I think," Henry sighs after a while, kissing her shoulder. "I'm going to give you a nice, warm bath."

I sweep her hair away from her neck and nuzzle into it. "And I'm going to change these sheets, then you can get back into them and get a good night's sleep."

"*We*," she whimpers, grabbing hold of my arm. "You're sleeping here, too."

"If that's what you want."

"That's what I want," she says, sleepily. "You already gave me the best present ever, but I want one more thing, and it's to fall asleep between both of you."

"Then that's what you'll get," Henry reassures her. "Merry Christmas, darling."

A deep sense of peace washes over me as I watch them kiss each other. This weekend was always going to be the end of something for me and my wife, but now it feels like it might also be the start of something new.

Henry's arm reaches for mine as Saskia rolls to face him. I curl my body around hers and wrap my arm around his back, not quite ready for any of us to leave the bed.

"Merry Christmas, angels."

Chapter 26

Henry

WARM FINGERS STROKE THROUGH my hair, pulling me slowly from the deepest sleep I've had in a long time.

The three of us fell asleep naked after taking turns to get clean last night. Unfortunately, the tiny cottage bathroom didn't allow us all to go in together, but visions of us in my walk-in shower in Manhattan danced through my dreams.

Getting to hold Saskia through the night is something I've wanted for a long time, but having Casper in bed with us too is something I never knew I would enjoy so much. The two of us wrapped our arms around her, and since the fire downstairs had died out long before, I was grateful for the extra warmth.

My eyes drift open, and when I realise they're Casper's fingers, I don't flinch like the first time he touched me, I just soften into it.

"Morning," he whispers. His eyes are still closed, so I'm not sure how he knew I was awake, but I smile and whisper back.

"Morning." There's a Saskia-shaped hole between us and I shuffle a little closer. "Where did she go?"

"Bathroom," he yawns, blinking himself into the present and looking up at me with those big brown eyes. With his long lashes, strong nose, and full lips, he's so fucking handsome, and I don't know how I never noticed.

I never noticed because I was too busy trying not to look at his wife.

"Are you OK?" he asks quietly. "About what happened, with us?"

The strangest thing is that it doesn't feel strange at all. I've never kissed another guy before last night, or touched anyone else's dick. Never thought it was something I particularly wanted to do, but once we started, I didn't want to stop.

"Pleasure is pleasure," I say, repeating his words from yesterday. "And I certainly had a lot of it last night."

"You've learned a few things." A coy smile spreads across his face, and I'd be tempted to roll my eyes, but he's right. He taught me a lot about Saskia, and a few new things about myself, too. I'll let him have the win. This time.

"I had a good teacher."

The fingers in my hair stroke down my cheek and come to a stop on my bare chest. "Still, we should have talked before, about you and I, not just our plans for her."

Curling my hand around his hip, I pull him even closer, smiling when I feel his erection nudge against my thigh.

"I'm fine, Casper. I promise, we didn't do anything I wasn't one hundred percent into."

"You're sure?"

"I'm sure. What you did for her was a gift for both of us. And I'm grateful for it."

The impulse to wrap my hand around his length is one I don't fight, then his mouth is back on mine, my own cock thickening as he reaches down between us.

By the time Saskia returns, Casper has me on my back, straddling my hips while we stroke each other off and lose ourselves in messy kisses.

"Get in here," I beckon, while he sucks at my throat.

"No, don't mind me," she says, pulling the chair from the corner to the foot of her bed. "I'm far too exhausted to play. You boys have fun and let me enjoy the show."

Chapter 27

Saskia

I FIGURED HENRY AND Casper would be exhausted after the amount of energy and attention they showered me with yesterday, so finding them jerking each other into a frenzy was a pleasant surprise.

After watching them come and helping them clean up, I let them fall back asleep, and made my way downstairs to deal with the aftermath of yesterday.

I can't contain my shock, muffling my giggles with my palm, when I take in the chaos of the living room. Lights still twinkle on the tree, illuminating a room that is strewn with clothes and sex toys.

Paper chains are still secured around each leg of the dining table, and I detach them carefully and drape what's still intact around the tree, knowing it will be a filthy reminder for the rest of our time here.

Yesterday was a far from traditional Christmas. We didn't even eat a proper meal, something I'm determined to remedy today. After getting the house back in order, I peel potatoes and carrots, and cover the turkey with a herb butter.

Once it's in the oven, I make a big cup of coffee, wrap up in my winter coat, and take it out to the small patio. Casper and I have shared many summer evenings here, chatting and eating and watching the sun set over the hills in the distance.

The snow is melting at last, and I sweep what's left off a chair before taking a seat at our little table and tipping my face to the sky.

This part of the country is beautiful at any time of year, but especially when sparkling in the low winter sun. A robin lands on the back of the other chair, its full red breast a circle of joy against the backdrop of white, green, and brown.

One would think that after several days of sex with your oldest friend and your ex-husband that your mind would be in a muddle, but I feel a deep sense of peace. There's no shame or angst churning in the pit of my stomach, no panic about where we go from here. Just peace and gratitude.

Two men have loved me, in their own ways, from near and far, for all of my adult life. I could not be luckier.

I'm halfway through my coffee when the door behind me clicks open, and Casper steps out, all dressed in his trademark black.

"The snow is melting," he says, taking the seat opposite me. "I'll probably be able to get back on the road today."

My heart sinks a little, even though deep down I've known this was inevitable. It's not like this can go on forever. Ultimately, the events of the past few days don't change anything between Casper and I. He still wants a family, and I don't. No amount of threesomes will convince me otherwise.

"I have another gift for you," he says, handing me a large manila envelope.

I slip it open, peek at the documents inside, and laugh. "Divorce papers? You shouldn't have."

My lawyer and I have already reviewed these multiple times, but one page is marked with a bright pink tab indicating changes. I scan them quickly, then read them again to make sure my eyes are not deceiving me.

"You're giving me the cottage? We agreed we'd split all the property assets."

"It was always yours, my love. You earned it. This proposes that you take the London flat, I'll take the house in Italy, and you can keep this place. Though you are welcome to visit any time, of course. You and Henry."

My eyes narrow and I shake my head. "I knew you were lying to me."

"About what?" he says, his eyebrows pulling together.

I point my finger close to his face. "You said you thought the cottage would be empty. Why did you bring these if you didn't think you were going to see me this Christmas?"

He leans forward with that wicked smile and playfully bites the tip.

"Fine, I admit I knew he would be here. I always had a sense that you would begin something with him once our marriage was over, but I wanted one last chance to say goodbye to you. I suspected, correctly I might add, that it might be an opportunity to give you the best present of all."

And what a gift it was.

"What if Henry hadn't been up for it?"

"Then we'd have had a very awkward few days trying to avoid each other in a tiny house." He reaches for my coffee and takes a sip. "We might have finished that jigsaw puzzle. Or watched Die Hard 2."

We both laugh, and it's the bright sound of our early years. Of fun and lightness and all the good times before we grew apart.

"I have met someone," he says after a while.

"Casper, no," I gasp. "Do not tell me you've made me complicit in an affair. Or Henry."

"Nothing has happened, but there is someone I was recently introduced to. She's a human rights lawyer in Italy, an incredible woman, almost as beautiful as you." He leans in to cover my hand with his. "I want to pursue her, with your blessing, of course."

"You don't need my blessing to start a new relationship."

He lifts my hand to his lips and presses a kiss to my knuckles. "I appreciate that, but you have been my closest companion for many years. You are my guiding light. My heart cannot simply forget you."

"You are annoyingly romantic sometimes. Of course you have my blessing. Do you have a pen?"

I sign the papers with a smile on my face, slip them back into the envelope, and hand it over.

"Saskia," he says softly, and my heart leaps into my throat.

From the moment we met, he has always called me *angel, my love,* or sometimes an Italian *tesoro*. In fact, it's so rare for him to use my name that I got the giggles when he said it during our marriage vows and had to stop for a sip of water.

He palms my cheek, and I lean into the warmth of it. "Henry is the one for you. You have my blessing, too."

"Thank you, Casper."

Our eyes lock, and he leans in to kiss me, but I pull away.

"Would you let me kiss you if Henry was here?" he asks, his eyes scanning my face to get a read on my reaction.

My lips press together as I consider the scenario. "I would, actually."

"That's interesting," he hums, standing and tucking the envelope underneath his arm. "I'm going to take a shower and pack up my things."

I watch him go, and wonder if I'll ever kiss my ex-husband again.

Chapter 28
Henry

CASPER AND I CLEANED up after the delicious lunch Saskia made for us, then he hit the road. It wasn't as awkward as I thought it might have been, all cordial handshakes and hugs bringing an end to our time together.

The house has been quiet since, but not in a bad way. Saskia and I move around each other with the ease of a couple who've been together for a long time. She prepares snacks, I top up wine glasses, and we sort puzzle pieces into piles at the dining table.

"Are you missing him?" she asks quietly, as the light outside fades to inky purples and blues.

"Oddly, yes, but I'm also delighted to have you to myself at long last." I reach out and steady her hand. "In fact, I think it's time we talked."

Saskia's back stiffens, panic written all over her face. It makes me even more nervous to tell her what I've been mulling over all morning.

"Actually, can we sit on the sofa? The other side of the table feels a million miles away."

We move and settle side by side, but I adjust her position, lifting her legs over my lap and taking a deep breath.

"So this trip hasn't exactly gone the way I thought it would."

"I know," she says, her head hanging low. "I'm sorry. The whole thing with Casper. He... I didn't—"

"You have nothing to be sorry for," I tell her. "It was just unexpected. I figured you and I would get reacquainted. Slowly. That we'd have a wonderful week together, then I'd fly home, and we'd spend the next year or two going back and forth between New York and London."

"You don't want that?"

"No. That's not an option for me now, and I knew that even before Casper turned up. I knew the second you opened the door on that first night, I wouldn't be able to say goodbye."

She looks straight at me with tears pricking at her lashes.

"Oh darling, don't cry."

"I thought you were about to tell me we don't stand a chance together. That this weekend was too much, and I'd scared you off."

"Too much? You're the perfect amount of everything, my love."

Her breath catches in her throat at the term of endearment.

"Is it OK to call you that? Because it's true. I love you, Saskia. I always have, in so many ways, but now I'm all in."

"I love you too," she says, pushing my hair back and tipping her lips to meet mine.

When our tongues collide, we shift to lie side by side on the sofa, and soon we are a tangle of limbs, pouring ourselves into each other, hands roaming and tugging as we strip out of our clothes. I pull her to the floor and we spend the best part of the evening making love right there in front of the fire.

"Here's what I think should happen," I tell her afterwards, snuggled up in blankets on the sofa, with her head on my chest. "I'll wind things up in Manhattan and move to London."

She props herself up on her elbows. "But you have a whole life in Manhattan."

"No," I say, shaking my head. "I have part of a life. The other part of my life is you, and it's always been missing. We can visit whenever we like, and I'll get my own place in London, so I won't be imposing on you."

"No," she says firmly.

"No?"

"I wouldn't want you to get your own place. We've wasted enough time."

I breathe a sigh of relief. "So I'll move in with you, and then I think perhaps we should join forces. Create a new art powerhouse. Hatton Stone."

"Hatton Stone?" she smiles, biting the side of her thumb. "I rather like that."

"So do I. And I know the ink is barely dry on your divorce papers, but I'd love if that was our name someday, too."

Saskia's face falls. "Do you want kids? It's been a long time since we've talked about it."

"I don't want anything you don't want."

"It's not that simple." She tries to pull away, but I shift positions to cradle her in my arms.

"Maybe with Casper it didn't seem that simple, but it's that simple for me. Nothing in the world matters to me more than you and your happiness."

She looks up at me with those wide blue eyes I know I want to spend the rest of my life getting lost in. "You'd give it all up for me?"

"In a heartbeat. I only ended up in New York because it was so painful to stay and see you soar with someone else by your side."

"Oh, Henry. Why didn't you say something?"

"What kind of friend would that have made me? I would never have stood in the way of your marriage. Which is why I won't dance around this any longer. I want to be with you, and I'll do anything to make it work, darling. You're my everything. The very best gift of all."

Chapter 29

Saskia

The Following Christmas

HENRY AND I DECORATED the tree yesterday, and the cottage looks as beautiful as ever. The fire is lit, carols are on the radio, but I'm too nervous to relax, hovering by the living room window and watching the skies.

"I hope this snow doesn't cause any problems on the roads."

Henry comes up behind me, wrapping his arms tightly around my waist. He has been nothing but a calming presence all year long, and I soften back against his chest.

"It will be fine," he says, sweeping my hair to one side and kissing my neck. "If we get snowed in like last year, I don't think that would be a bad thing."

"What if we don't have enough food?"

"Darling, that fridge will burst if you put another thing in it. We have more than enough food, and I've put extra bottles of Champagne in the garden to keep cool. If it's anything like our summer trip, we won't spend much time eating, anyway. Well... not food."

His warm laugh sends a shiver down my spine. He sinks his teeth into my neck, and my thighs squeeze together.

Henry moved to London in March, and our art dealership, House of Hatton Stone, launched soon after. Casper's millionaire Mayfair client bragged about his recent commissions in Architectural Digest, so it's been a great year for him too.

In July, we spent a heavenly week in Italy visiting him and his new girlfriend, Lucilla. Fortunately for all of us, she has a similar attitude when it comes to sex. *'Pleasure is pleasure'*, and we should seek as much of it as possible.

After talking about it on the phone beforehand, then again in person, we agreed we were all open to experimenting together and planned to see where the mood took us.

We barely made it past dinner on the first night before our men turned their chairs to face each other and lifted us into their respective laps. They unbuttoned our summer dresses, hooked our legs open, and placed bets on which woman could make herself orgasm first.

I was far too distracted watching Lucilla play with her beautiful body to win, but from there, it was pretty clear we'd be spending our week as a foursome in various states of ecstasy. She and I have become good friends since, and speak often.

"Aren't you nervous?" I ask him.

"More excited than nervous. Last year was so amazing. It's a lot to live up to."

"What part do you think about most?" I ask, catching a cheeky smile spreading across his face when I turn in his arms.

"Strangely, it's the getting out of the cuffs part after you left us tied to those chairs."

I glance past his shoulder at the dining table and try not to laugh. Those chairs took a beating last year, and the table needed a thorough clean-up after what they did to me on it.

"You never did tell me how you managed it."

"Teamwork, darling." He kisses one cheek, then the other. "What was your favourite part?"

"The fullness," I sigh, a dull ache blooming between my legs. "That sensation of being filled everywhere. I couldn't think about anything except how good it felt."

My god, the fullness.

I think about it often.

"Well, then I'm glad we have some extra toys this year to help us all feel that way."

Henry and I have spent a lot of the past twelve months experimenting with all the ways we can make each other feel good.

The box of toys on the dining table now contains a few strap-on toys of various sizes. All December, my thoughts have drifted to fantasies about me and Lucilla watching each other fuck our men while they kiss, and I know she's been thinking about it, too.

I'm also hoping she and I will find ourselves tied back to back like the boys were last year. Perhaps also blindfolded for an even more intense game of Guess Who?

Suddenly, there are headlights on the approach, and the room floods with light. I can hardly contain my excitement when Casper's car comes to a stop in the driveway, and two beautiful figures step out.

"They're here."

Henry cups my face and kisses me deeply. It's one last moment that's just for us. I feel his cock getting hard already, and wonder how long it will be before the fun and games begin.

"Come on," he says, guiding me towards the door. "Let's make this Christmas even better than the last."

THE END

Acknowledgements

This book would not exist without my Book Babes, the beloved friends who joined me for a reading retreat in 2023 that turned out to be one of the best weekends of my life.

When I, well rested thanks to an enormous bed in a country manor, woke up and said *'I had an idea for a threesome book in the night'*, they did not bat an eyelid. Instead, they made me a coffee and sat me down to write.

I have barely rested since.

Thank you to my wonderful readers, I hope you love this little surprise novella as much as I think you will.

Thank you to my character artist, Irdeinfierno, and my cover artist Melissa at Mel D Designs for the amazing cover.

Thank you to my wonderful PA, Brooke, for endless encouragement and secret-keeping.

Thank you to Aldi for your Lightly Sea Salted Hand Cooked Crisps, of which I have consumed about 400 million this year.

And thank you to Alex, for everything, always.

Also By Holly June Smith

Can I Tell You Something?

Hannah Richmond is about to spend Christmas with the man of her dreams. The man of Hannah's dreams has no idea she exists.

—ele—

Hannah

I've been desperately looking forward to Christmas in my family's snowy alpine chalet. Two blissful weeks of skiing, eating, and sneaking off for *'naps'* to listen to my favourite audio erotica star.

Yes, the man who warms my bed each night may have no idea I exist, but that doesn't stop me fantasising that his spicy stories and filthy words are for my ears only.

It's set to be the most relaxing Christmas ever. Until my brother shows up... with an unexpected guest.

Cameron

I'd planned to spend the holidays working. Just me, my microphone, and a lot of new content for subscribers of my audio erotica channel.

When I convinced my best friend to fly home and surprise his family, I never expected he'd take me along for the ride. I didn't expect to find myself halfway up a mountain. And I definitely didn't expect to find out his sister is my biggest fan.

Chapter One

For as long as I can remember, Christmas has always meant three things: snow, skiing, and sugar cookies.

Ever since I was a baby, my family has spent Christmas and New Year at my grandma's chalet in the French Alps. The first thing we'd do when we arrived in the sleepy mountain village was head straight to the *patisserie* for cookies. And since my brother, Ryan, isn't joining us this year, *again*, that means I'll get to eat them all by myself.

At least, that's the positive spin I'm putting on spending Christmas alone with my parents.

I could stay in London, but the thought of waking up in my poky little flat alone on Christmas morning is too depressing. My grandma is sadly no longer with us, and though Dad suggested I bring a friend, I've been working so hard I haven't been keeping up with my social circle much. Plus, it's always been *our place*. I wouldn't love it so much if I were hyper analysing our annual traditions through the eyes of an interloper.

Truthfully, I need this trip, and I need a break. My first year as a lawyer has been intense, and I feel guilty about taking time off. The workload will only get heavier, so I don't know if I'll be able to visit the mountains again after this year. Ryan certainly finds it difficult now that he's working out in L.A.

My brother moved to California for film school a few years ago, and now he's working hard to make a name for himself in TV production.

In fact, he's working so hard he didn't make it home last year, nor the year before that, and he's not making this one either. Which means I haven't seen my brother in three years, and... ugh. I swallow hard and fix a smile on my face as I inch along in the queue.

I know that's what's really getting me down, but I can't push the thought away. A lifetime of Christmases in the happiest place in the world will soon become a distant memory. No more competing for top speed, no stuffing ourselves with fondue, and no sledging home from dinner in the dark.

It's the end of an era, another thing outside of my control. Much like the dark clouds threatening to delay my flight.

London City airport is packed with businessmen frantically typing and aggressively shouting into their phones as they shuffle their way through long security lines. I swear this is the most testosterone filled airport in the country, and every briefcase owner in London is escaping for winter break.

I briefly wonder where all their luggage is, before remembering I'm amongst the one percent here. Men who aren't quite wealthy enough to justify a private jet, but likely have holiday homes stocked with every outfit they could possibly need, including the latest winter sports gear. And a driver to collect them once we land in Geneva, of course.

I can hardly judge them. I am off to my family's chalet after all, but ours is small by Alpine standards. My ski gear lives there all year round, but I've still had to cram everything I need into my cabin sized bag, lest I get stiffed for fees on both legs of the journey. Fortunately, it's mostly comfy loungewear and I'll enjoy a visit to a French pharmacy to stock up on toiletries and skincare.

After collecting my hand luggage from security, thankfully without being stopped for an extra bag check, I weave my way through the Duty Free shop.

I'm tempted by a giant Toblerone. We used to beg Dad to buy them for us, but he always refused and told us the artisanal, handmade chocolates we could buy in the mountains would be worth the wait. He wasn't wrong, and I've been a snob about chocolate ever since, but those chunky triangles still have a certain allure.

Gin, however, that I certainly will need if I'm to survive two weeks alone with parents who will only want to talk about my career plans and lack of relationship status. I can hardly wait to be ambushed before I've even taken off my coat. I pay for two bottles of Malfy and scroll Instagram as I weave through the crowds.

The departures board has no gate listed, so I'm early enough for a glass of champagne and a spot of people watching. After ordering, I nab a high stool along the bar that faces out towards the crowds and settle in.

Several extremely attractive men stroll by. There are those in suits and tailored wool coats, others in dark jeans that hug them in all the right places, shirt buttons open at the collar just so. Some are alone, others are in a group, frenetic chatter that suggests they're also about to kick back and enjoy some downtime together. One man catches my eye as he walks towards me, a dazzling smile spread across his clean-shaven face.

A girl could do well for herself in a place like this. A girl with confidence and charisma, that is. I'm cursed to flush beetroot red and look down at my feet until he passes me by.

My dating life is abysmal, and that's nobody's fault but my own. I've dabbled with apps, and agreed to being set up a few times, but no man can scratch my particular itch.

The truth is, I have deep-rooted trust issues. That and I'm already in all-consuming love with a man who lives on the other side of the world, has no idea I exist, and makes me come multiple times a night.

And if I want him, as I often do, all I have to do is push in my earbuds, and there he is, ready to whisper the most delicious filth straight into my ears.

You see, the man of my dreams is American audio erotica voice actor, *Mac'n'Please*.

In my search for sexual stimulation a little less aggressive than mainstream pornography, I found audio porn on Reddit a couple of years ago. Entire libraries of creators work featuring every fantasy you could ever think of, plus plenty I could never have come up with on my own. There are sexy stories, creator confessions, guided masturbation tutorials, and even comfort audios to soothe you into a blissful sleep. I can't tell you exactly what drew me to Mac, except that after two minutes of listening to his voice, I was more turned on than I'd ever been with any man in real life.

I've been shamefully addicted ever since. Not that seeking sexual gratification is anything to be ashamed of, but it's not the sort of thing you bring up at parties. Though at this point, I'd rather spend my evenings at home listening to men moaning than pretending to be confident enough for parties.

Me: Just boarded

Ryan: Safe travels

My brother's blunt replies are a new thing, mostly caused by a heavy workload. When we both lived at home, our parents couldn't shut us up. Now, I'm half convinced I'd never hear from him if I didn't force him to call me and check in once a week.

Me: Sure I can't change your mind?

Ryan: Afraid not. Work is crazy busy right now

Me: More chocolate for me then

The first Christmas he missed, I was seriously pissed off, but I can't be mad when I know he's working so hard at a job that he loves.

My seatbelt securely in place, I impatiently watch the safety briefing. The second it's over, I connect my bluetooth headphones, find my favourite *Mac'n'Please* audio, and hit play.

Continue reading: Can I Tell You Something?

Made in the USA
Las Vegas, NV
08 December 2024

13651878R00094